CW00872215

# Red Mirror

# Red Mirror

Kingdom Chronicles Book 4

*Jesse Wilson*

# Chapter One

Larenville, Vanir.

Cornell Nightworth was annoyed. The sun was already hot out here and even if he lived his whole life in the desert, being out of Echemos was always considerably worse, maybe it was all in his head. The people with the cameras found themselves way out here in middle of the hot sand, anything for a chance at a grim tale to entertain the masses. "Get those media parasites out of here," he said with a fair amount of anger in his voice, finally hitting his tolerance limit.

"You got it, boss," someone replied from farther away and started to move the crowd back by pushing the magical barrier line further back. "Do you think this has any connection to the Unicorn attack in Naber?" some reporter asked and Cornell stopped and looked over at the man. "No," he replied quietly as they were pushed away. He was pretty sure a unicorn had nothing to do with this.

"I can see it now, Mystic Force Detective slaughters innocent reporters after they asked really dumb questions," Jenny said with a slight laugh, she was wearing a dark suit, her golden badge on the left side. Her black hair and brown eyes reflected the sunlight with an unnatural intensity. "Oh, that'd be fun but we all know reporters never really die, they just respawn from the infinite void," Cornell replied, trying not to laugh and look professional in the presence of the public and looked forward towards the crime scene all the same.

He brushed the red dust away from his white shirt, wondering to himself why he chose to wear white in a place like this. He was sure no one was going to question him about it. Right now, no one wanted to attract attention to themselves, no one normal anyway.

"Same old questions, but no answers. Why would a Necromancer death squad come to this no name desert town?" he asked as he looked over the bodies of the victims as they all lay where they were discovered. Six elves had been stripped naked and dismembered. Three men and three women on display as if they were some twisted art project. Cornell swallowed his disgust for the people who did this. Instead he tried to focus on the details.

"I have no idea, but look. No blood, it looks like they were freeze dried or something," she said but couldn't make sense of it. In a scene like this there should have been a lot, everywhere. "Yeah, that was the first thing I noticed. Do we know who any of these people are yet?" Cornell asked, hoping she got some new information. "Not a clue. Six random elves who apparently had a grudge with someone, this could be a mob hit," Jenny suggested the only thing she could think of.

"Out here, in this place. What would the Moreno family want way out here in a place like this? This isn't their style. Then again, its clear these people weren't killed here either," Cornell replied and continued. "They were either dropped out of the sky, or teleported in. My guess is teleportation, we didn't find any tracks. It's not windy and check it out, the only footsteps around us are our own," Cornell said as another picture was taken.

Then a van started to drive down the road and came to a stop. "The meat wagon's here," Jenny replied, turned and looked. She brushed her black hair out of her face as a few strands got loose. "Come on, let's talk a few of these people, see what we can find out. We're not going to learn anything new staring at these bodies," Cornell said and tore his gaze off of the grisly scene in front of him.

"Yeah, I don't think we'll get much out of these people. The desert communities like this are all pretty quiet," she replied as the coroners began to approach. Cornell nodded then turned to them. "Make sure you don't lose any pieces and keep the bodies together," he said to them. "This isn't our first day, we got this. Don't worry about it," the leader of the group replied. Cornell didn't appreciate the attitude, but chose to ignore it.

"Alright. We'll split up. I'll take Risbu's general store and you go for, well, you know what to do," Cornell replied. She smiled at him. "I wouldn't be here if I didn't," she replied and the two of them walked their separate directions.

Risbu's general store wasn't anything special, he had seen a thousand places just like it before in countless other towns before this one. "Hello, Detective. How can I help you today?" an old elf said and came walking from out of the back. He was dressed in a blue shirt with black jeans, they weren't anything special but for a place like this it was pretty normal. Cornell decided to get right to the point and skip the small talk.

"Yeah, did you see anything that might help with what happened out there?" Cornell asked, he knew this guy wasn't a good suspect, but there was no reason to be hostile about anything yet.

"Those bodies out there, you mean? Oh. I sleep upstairs. I was in bed a couple hours after dark. I didn't see anything. But sometime just before the sunrise I heard a weird, I don't know, slurping sound?" the man said and Cornell had no idea what that might have been. "No clocks upstairs, what time was it when you heard the sound. Anything can help," he replied.

The old elf laughed. "Oh, about three in the morning I'd say," he replied and looked out the window. "I haven't seen anything like it since the war," he said off hand, his voice trailing off. The last war was before Cornell's time, about twenty years. "What do you mean?" he asked.

"It's an old vampire terror tactic, they would kidnap our buddies in the dark and return them in pieces, sucked dry," Risbu replied and shuddered. "I don't like talking about it much. You know, it's all terrible," he said, voice not as strong. "Vampires, have there been any around we can talk to?" Cornell replied as he raised an eyebrow.

"I didn't serve for fifty years in the Last Light Alliance just so I could turn around and serve those razor tooth freaks, there are no vampires in Larenville. It's why I moved to the Vanir. Most sunlight of any of the kingdoms, it keeps most of them clear," he said with anger.

"Alright old timer, relax. I didn't mean to bring up anything. I just need to find every answer," Cornell asked, but now he felt like the old man knew more than he was telling. "No, I don't know anything else. I don't know why some maniacs would show up here and leave their work like it was some kind of art project. But I didn't see anything, but the camera might have," Risbu replied and started moving towards the counter.

Cornell followed him. "Well let's see the footage," he replied and Risbu nodded. He got behind the counter and pushed a few buttons. A screen popped up out of it. "I'll play the last few hours," he said and pushed the button. Cornell watched. All it showed was the inside of the store. Seeing anything from this angle was going to be almost impossible.

Risbu sped up the footage to just before three in the morning. Neither of them saw anything that had changed. "Are you sure about what time you heard it?" Cornell asked, already getting a little impatient. Just before the old man answered, the outside windows flashed with bright purple light. There was no sound but the light only lasted a few seconds. "I swear I never saw any light like that. I just heard that weird sound," Risbu replied. Cornell didn't believe him, but that was just part of the job.

"Can I keep this footage?" he asked and the man looked at him. "Do you have a warrant?" Risbu asked right back. Cornell narrowed his eyes just a little, his frustration was rising. "Kidding, young Elf, take it. If it helps put the people behind this away I'll sleep easier," Risbu said with a laugh. Cornell didn't want to play games today, his sense of humor was wearing thin already this hot morning.

"Thank you, and if you remember anything, call me," Cornell said and a white business card appeared in his hand. "Sure, the name is Andy Risbu, if I call at least you'll know my name," he said. Cornell nodded as Risbu handed him the disc that was in the machine. Cornell took it and, smiled and started walking towards the door.

"Not even a thanks, damn kids today," Andy said mostly to himself as Cornell walked out of the building.

Jenny had her own theories. There was a crowd of villagers gathering just outside the barrier line. She put on her best smile and walked towards the crowd. "Does anyone know anything?" she asked the crowd as she walked in their direction. "Anything can help, any detail, any ideas, theories, leads. Anything," she said again as she approached the crowd.

No one was too eager to say anything. "We don't talk to Pixies," someone yelled out from the back. "Who said that?" Jenny asked and stared into the crowd with her deep brown eyes. No one answered.

"I am a Mystic Force Detective. I am one of the only people who gives a damn about protecting you out here way out in the middle of this dusty wasteland. The people who did this, they can come back at anytime and do it again, so I ask you again, what one of you inbred hicks decided that now was a good time to be a loudmouthed idiot?" she asked again with force. Her black hair began to shimmer with golden energy as the anger grew.

"Okay, it was me," a man came walking through the crowd. He was and older elf dressed in a red shirt and blue jeans. His green eyes narrowed at her as he came into view. "Great, why?" she asked in a hurry. "Pixies are evil, you are evil. You shouldn't be here," he replied and she shook her head. "You elves, I swear you get worse every year. Tell you what, if you decide to tell me what you know. I'll leave and you'll never see me again. If you don't. If you hold anything back I will make sure a whole horde of Pixies just like me come down and scour every single piece of evidence out of this place we can get, come clean now," Jenny said and the man swallowed, the fear in his green eyes was easily seen.

"I don't, I swear I don't know anything. Drank last night at the Arrow and Quiver. I woke up just a couple of hours ago," he said and Jenny rolled her eyes. "Okay, how about anyone else. Surely someone saw something," Jenny said again. Hoping to get some kind of a lead.

"I did," someone said, someone young. Jenny turned her attention to the barely thirteen-year-old elf. She walked to her. "What did you see?" she asked. "It was a man. He was dressed all in green. It was only for a split second. He made a weird movement his hands. There was a purple light. The...they appeared on the ground as you see them now," she said, trying to remember everything. "Then the green man left," she said and Jenny needed more.

"How tall, old, anything you can remember," she asked, trying to soften her voice then. "No, the green was like a cloak. I saw nothing. But he was about as tall as him," she pointed. Jenny turned and looked only to see Cornell walking in her direction. "Thanks," she replied and walked over to him.

"Get anything useful?" she asked. "Just some bad video footage of a strange purple light," he said and she nodded. "Yeah. Someone saw a person all in green doing some magic, but that's about it," Jenny replied and Cornell shook his head. "Well this whole thing is likely a message of some kind, but is it for us, or for this whole town? I guess we'll be stuck here for a while to try and figure it all out," he said. "Damn it," she replied, feeling a whole lot less comfortable after her last encounter.

"Don't be so upset about it, it could be worse. We could be assigned to the Outside," he replied and she nodded. "Alright, we'll set up at the hotel, hope its not a complete disaster. Then we see what we can find out from there," she said and Cornell nodded. It was a good as plan as any.

# Chapter Two

In Larenville, there was only one place to stay. A place called the Pleasant Dream Inn. It wasn't always a place to stay, that was easy to tell by the looks of it. It was two stories high and each room appeared to have a window. The place was a light green and it stood out intentionally with the mostly red surrounding dirt. The sign was old and the paint was cracked due to exposure from the elements.

The two of them walked through the front door, there was a young elf girl in an equally green uniform there at the front desk "Hello," she said just as cheerfully as she would any other customer, smiled too. "I don't trust this one," Cornell said under his breath. Jenny narrowed her eyes and took over.

"Yeah, we'll need one room for an unspecified amount of time," she said and a black card appeared in her hand and she put it on the desk. The desk clerk took it. "Oh my, Mystic Force cards are pretty rare around these parts," she said and put it through the slider. A second later the computer beeped. "Looks like everything is in order, you'll be in room eighteen, just let us know when you're ready to check out," she said and Cornell nodded as the key cards were handed over. They both took one and started down the hall towards their room.

The desk clerk narrowed her eyes as they walked down the hall and turned out of sight. She picked up the phone and dialed a number. "Yeah, those Detectives aren't leaving town anytime soon. They are staying here," she said quietly. "Alright, you got it," she said and hung up the phone.

Cornell and Jenny made there way into the room. The place was about as basic as rooms came. "Man, I hope the air unit isn't broken," Cornell said looking around, he didn't even see anything to make the room cooler. "Don't worry about it, nothing a little magic can't fix," Jenny replied. "Lome" she said and with a wave of her hand the sweltering heat of the room melted away and it was comfortable again. "See, I got it covered," she said and smiled.

"Thanks," Cornell replied and looked out the window. From here he could see where they found the bodies. "Any idea of where to start looking?" Jenny asked. "Not even one, but we know someone doesn't like elves, they picked here for a reason and someone in green did it," Cornell replied. It wasn't much to go on but it was a start.

"And they don't like Pixies, either," she said and shook her head. "Yeah, not everyone is over the war, especially the elves. It takes a long time for people to get over stuff like that," he replied and knew this was going to be a tough case to crack. "But who cares what these people think. We have a job to do," he finished. "First thing is to find out who the victims were and what their connection to this town is," she said and he nodded.

"The coroner's tent is only a mile outside of town, it's hidden. They won't have any information yet," she said and got an idea. "I wonder if this a revenge thing, six elves drained in a dead end town, this place has to mean something to the one who did this," she added. "I'll ask around town, see what I can dig up," she said and smiled.

"No, you go to the coroner tent and see if they have anything, if they don't make them work harder. Your presence here has already riled up the locals more than enough. No matter what form you take they'll be looking for you. Let them forget a little bit," Cornell said and she glared at him. "Trust me on this one. I'll ask around, you find out who the dead ones are," he repeated. "Fine," she replied and disappeared in a plume of sparkling gold dust and disappeared into nothing as it hit the floor.

Cornell took a look around the room and walked towards the door. As he walked towards the door. He tossed a silver coin on the floor in a far corner, it landed with the bird facing up. Then he left the room and walked back down the hall. The girl behind the desk wasn't there anymore, he'd question her later.

He walked out of the inn and straight back into the sun and heat. The village was as quiet as it was before, maybe even a little more. Right now, the place almost looked abandoned. The old man in the store was already questioned, but maybe there were other cameras that got a better point of view of what happened. Cornell wasn't going to believe the story about anything without some evidence. It could have all been made up from the wild imagination of a teenager, or a deliberate attempt to throw them off the trail.

Cornell walked to another business, Red King's Diner, it was called. However, when he got the door there was a notice made out of bright orange paper on it and he read it. "Closed for town meeting, will reopen in one hour," he said as he read it and he was curious. Looking up and down the street, every business around had a similar notice on the door. "Are you serious right now, the whole town shut down, but where did everyone go?" he asked and looked up the road. Like most small towns in the desert, all the main businesses were on the main road in the center.

At the far end was a church dedicated to the Goddess Loa. It was old and stained with the red dust of the ages. It also appeared big enough to hold everyone in town. There was only one place they could have been, so he began to walk down the road.

Something about the place was making him feel off. He had been to hundreds of places just like this, but none of them had ever been like this in the middle of the day before. It was strange.

Cornell made it to the church and put his hand around the handle of the door, then he stopped and looked around. No one was watching him, and his natural elf senses didn't detect anyone sneaking about or standing guard.

"I'll see what this meeting is all about," he said and took his hand off the door, walked to the side. He pulled out a copper coin and held it against the wall. In a few seconds he could hear the low murmur of a crowd inside.

"Alright, everyone please sit down," a woman's voice said. Cornell supposed that this was the Mayor of the town, or something like it. There was a shuffling of feet and everything went quiet. "Let this meeting come to order," she said and Cornell was already getting tired of standing here and wished they'd get on with it.

"As you know we have had a tragic event in this town and we have two Detectives poking around," she said, and continued. "I want you all to tell them everything they need to know," she said and Cornell thought that was strange. Why would she say it like that?

"What about the Pixie?" someone yelled out in anger. "Listen, I know you're all upset about that. All we can do is endure it until they go away. If we tell them everything we know about it, they'll go away that much sooner," she replied to the man.

"Who even called Mystic Force, we have our own cops. Someone in this room is a traitor," a deep voice cried out. "I don't know who called them, but it doesn't matter," the woman in charge replied. "They'll all be gone soon enough," she said.

"So just act natural and relax. If they ask about the meeting, tell them it was a vigil or something for the victims, if they ask why, just say it was tradition for the dead," she said. Cornell wondered if there was some kind of town secret, why they all had to be reminded not to say anything about it he wasn't too sure.

"But just for a little reinforcement," she said. "Halivate" she said and the magic of his listening coin and whatever spell she just cast had a horrible feed back effect. The screeching noise made him step back from the wall. "Memory blocker?" Cornell asked himself. He was familiar with the spell. Low life criminals used it to erase memories, but it only lasted a few days at the most.

He learned something. First, someone in authority of the town knew magic, and second, everyone was in on a bigger secret. But that didn't mean it was something illegal, but now he didn't know if it was connected to this case or not. Also, this woman blocked everyone's memories without their permission. Cornell could have arrested her for that, but that would ruin everything. He planned to follow this and see where the trail led.

"Alright everyone, that concludes our meeting, don't forget to come to services tonight," she said in a totally different tone of voice. Then the low murmur of the crowd picked up and he could hear footsteps starting to move towards the door. Not wanting to be seen by anyone he walked to the back of the building. He leaned against the wall and crossed his arms, started to think about what to do from here.

# Chapter Three

Jenny appeared in the tent just outside of town in golden plume of dust. No one was startled by her appearance. "Tell me you have something that we can use as a lead," she said, getting the point. "Lots of things, and at the same time nothing," Dorf replied. Dorf was a Dwarf in a white protection suit with dark blue gloves.

"Out with it, I am in no mood for games," she said and he looked at her. "Are you ever?" he asked and brought his attention back to the bodies on the table. "Aside from the obvious, we don't know how they were drained. We didn't find any puncture marks on the body. We assume that the pieces were drained one at a time," he said.

"What kind of maniac does that?" she asked and Dorf just shrugged. "No idea, but who or what ever it was did really nice work. I mean look at the edges. If I didn't know better I'd say a this was a Razorhorn's art project or something," he said and continued. "We do know these elves never worked much, nor were they even from here. The sand people are no where near this pale. There isn't anything on the missing persons line yet so who knows who they are," he finished.

"Any magic energy on them?" Jenny asked, she knew there still had to be something. "Yeah, a low level teleport spell most second or third year mages could do. That doesn't help us much, but it does give us a range estimate," he said. "Yeah, ten miles is the limit for the basic port spells, if it was. Cornell said he has footage of a weird purple light so it could be a proxy spell, too," she said. Dorf frowned.

"If it was, it's impossible to know where it came from. But Proxy spells are really hard to pull off, so if it is, we are looking for a graduated mage or something bigger. Vanir keeps track of all the mages so that might narrow the list a little," Dorf said. "I'll get looking into that. Do you know anything about this place Larenville? Why do they hate Pixies so much?" Jenny asked.

Dorf looked away. "History is such a pain in the neck," he said. "Come on, tell me. It would make my life easier," she replied. "I doubt it, listen. It was a century ago. I think you should just let it go, endure the annoyance and get out. If you really want to know just, well, look up the history on your own. Not the government standard stuff though, look deeper," Dorf said and looked away.

Jenny didn't know what to think of all that but decided it wasn't that important. "Alright, whatever. I'm going to get started and see what mages are able to cast a port spell like that. If you find out anything else about the victims, let me know," she said and walked away, moved towards a computer station on the wall.

Police work was the worst part of the job. Digging through endless lists, notes and all the lies people liked to tell was tedious to say the least. She sat down at the chair and quickly logged in under her name and looked up the mage registration list. The majority of the list were the new mages and beginners. Those part of the lists she closed out. The one she was looking for could pull off some pretty impressive tricks so she refined her search. Jenny typed in the search box at the top, Proxy.

The first one on the list was the Henne Ashe, Arch mage of the Cosmic Flame and head master of the Yondo Tower. Jenny was sure this one would easily be capable of doing something like this but, there was little to motive for it. Unless the mage was secretly insane or something and no one knew it, she could cut this one off the list, maybe.

The next one on the list was Master Zincol Roud. Royal Mage of Vanir. This guy rarely ever left Arket Palace. There was little reason to suspect him in this madness either. Both of these locations were nowhere near village anyway, it would have been a massive waste of energy to teleport such a vast distance to dump some bodies, besides, why would you leave them in the middle of a village. That didn't make any sense.

The last one on this short list was a name called Professor Zozo. Former Leader of the Firewalkers, exiled due to unethical experiments. Believed to be dead. Jenny read almost out loud and rolled her eyes.

"Well if anyone screams I'm a bad guy, this is it. Too bad we don't know where he is," she said and decided that enough time was spent hanging around the dead things. It was time to head back to town. Jenny disappeared in that same plume of golden dust.

Seconds later she reformed in their hotel room. It looked just like they left it. Cornell wasn't back yet, however, her eye went right to the silver coin. It was procedure to place them in any room to make sure no one had broken into it. However, the coin was dragon side up. Someone had been in here and it wasn't them. Jenny cursed her luck, she didn't think that would happen so soon but who ever it was, didn't know about the coin. Not many people did.

Jenny walked over to the coin and was about to pick it up when the door opened. She turned around to see Cornell walking inside. He was about to say something when she pointed at the coin, showing it was turned over. Cornell rolled his eyes but then motioned her to press it.

She did and all at once the coin shot green beams of light over every surface. Then the playback began. The two of them watched as the woman behind the counter came in to the room. She was holding some kind of small device and moved towards the light in the center of the room. Then she proceeded to step on the bed and place the thing inside the glass cover, it disappeared after a button was pressed. She carefully got off the bed, straightened out the blanket and quickly left, locking the door behind her. Cornell opened the door back up and motioned for Jenny to follow. The two of them left the room.

"Bugged," Jenny said and Cornell nodded. "Yeah, if we take it out, whomever is listening will know, so we play it like we don't know. Write anything down important and play stupid," he said and she sighed. They both hated stuff like this. "Don't worry, I know a guy who's going to help," he said with a smile and Jenny groaned.

"Fine, just don't do too much damage," she said and rolled her eyes. "No worries," he replied with a smile, opened the door and motioned for her to go in first. She did and he followed her in. "So, do you have any leads?" Cornell asked and she looked at him. "Yes, and now. We know a high level mage had to do the teleporting, but all the ones with the know how are leagues away. We'll find out who did it," she replied. Telling him nothing, but saying everything.

Quickly with a pen and paper on the desk she wrote Zozo's name on it and held it up to him. He read it and nodded. "Well, everything will be revealed in time, we will just have to look a little harder. I'm convinced someone in this town knows something," Cornell said with a smile. "And we'll find out who it is," he finished, but he knew that name already. He pretended he didn't, at least for now.

The two of them sat down on the chairs on both ends of the desk. Neither of them knew why there were two chairs in the room but it was pointless to question that now. "Lets just wait until after dark and mingle, see what comes up," Jenny replied with a smile.

"I'm sure there is lots to learn," he replied and looked out the window. From here all he could see was endless desert, not a single sign of life anywhere. Cornell had no idea why anyone would want to live way out here in a wasteland.

# Chapter Four

The bright sun fell out of the sky in just a few hours and it was tolerable to go outside again. The two of the changed into more causal clothes. "Think we will learn anything out there?" she asked. "Who knows but I know we won't learn anything in this room, let's go," he said and the two of them walked out of the room and down the hall.

The person behind the front desk was an older elf and he looked like he was half asleep to them. Ignoring him they made their way back outside. The night air was cool and brisk, the scent on the wind was almost sweet. Neither of them knew where that was coming from.

"The Arrow and Quiver, right, that's what one of the guys said?" Cornell asked and she stared at him. "Some detective you are, forgetting random details like that," she replied, he laughed a little bit. "Come on, let's go," he replied and shook his head a little.

The Arrow and Quiver was an easy place to find. It was the only place that appeared to be open after the sun went down and even though there was a mysterious event that happened, the bar was as busy as ever.

"It looks like half the town is here, literally," Jenny said as they walked up to the place. "Yep," Cornell replied, but most of the small towns out here in the desert were the same way. One place to gather for fun, another for emergencies and worship. Larenville was no different. The two of them walked inside and if anyone noticed them, there was no way to tell.

Smoke filled the bar, the music played something that must have been popular around here. Neither of them had ever heard it before. Most of the people here were sitting around at tables. A few were playing darts off to the side, others playing pool. Everyone had a drink in their hand and appeared to be having a great time.

Cornell figured this had more to do with the memory blocking spell than anything. There was no way a group of people could be this happy, even if they didn't know who the victims were. "Yeah, the town had a meeting, someone cast a memory block on everyone who was there, I don't know what she was trying to block out if no one knew anything about the crime," he said and Jenny shrugged.

"Let's mingle, if we whisper to one another like this all night someone's going to get suspicious, meet you back at the room and please try not to bring anyone home. There is only one bed and I don't like sharing on the job," she said with a glare. "I'll do my best, not like last time I swear," he said, smiled as he turned and walked away from her. She didn't like to think about last time and cringed a little. Then figured nothing would happen anyway due to the room being bugged.

Cornell walked straight to the bar and was lucky enough to find an empty seat. He sat down there, the bartender was there in just a few seconds. "Hey, what can I get you?" she asked and he shrugged. "Something that won't kill me or make me go blind," he said with a smile and she nodded. "I got just the thing, you can't be too careful in these desert towns," she said and picked up on his sense of humor pretty fast.

She came back with a bottle of red rum and a glass, setting them both down at the same time. "You're that detective, right?" she asked and he nodded. "Usually, right now, I am just off duty normal guy. Getting the feel for this town and trying to get assimilated a little bit. People open up if you're not a dick, you know?" he said and she smiled. "Yeah, that's true. Any leads yet?" she asked, catching him by surprise.

"A couple, always a couple things rolling around," he replied, not sure where to go with this. If she was asking about the case, that had to mean that this elf wasn't at the meeting today. "Good, I hope that find out who did it. That was just insane," she replied as his glass was filled up carefully with something dark green. "I heard there was a town meeting today, it was on all the storefronts around here, any idea what it was about?" he asked.

She shrugged. "I couldn't go, I was stuck prepping the kitchen for tonight, no one else felt good enough to show up for work and I almost closed, but then they came back after the meeting, feeling better. I didn't ask why. It was strange," she replied. He wanted to ask more but suddenly someone on the other end of the bar started shouting for a refill. "Duty calls, enjoy the rum its on the house," she replied and walked away. Cornell watched her go with a smile.

Then carefully took a sip, trying to detect toxins. He didn't smell anything. "Oh, what the hell," he said to himself and drank it. It burned all the way down but tasted like cinnamon, it was strong and it made his eyes water a little. He didn't show it as he looked around the room, looking for anyone else that might seem out of place. So far everything appeared normal.

Jenny walked into the crowd and despite the aggression from earlier. No one seemed to even recognize her right now or at the very least care all that much. "Hey there, you, yeah, can I buy you a drink?" some guy asked and came up from behind. "Well, sure that'd be kind of you," she replied with a smile. "Cool, I'll be right back, you'll see," he said and it was clear that he was already half drunk.

"Caine hits on anything that moves, he's the type to tell every woman he ever sees that she's the most beautiful thing he's ever seen…until the next one comes along," another voice said, standing beside her. "Oh, well, I guess that doesn't make me very special," she said and frowned a little. Jenny didn't care one way or another, once this case was solved this place was going to be in the rear view mirror and history forever.

"No, I suppose it doesn't," he replied and continued. "Name's Joe, and you're new here. A pixie no less. What brings a Pixie like you to a high elf town like this?" Joe asked. The memory block must have been powerful, Jenny just shrugged. "Oh, just exploring Vanir and found myself here," she said, sometimes memory blocks could be removed with hints to real memories, she didn't want to risk it. "But Larenville, after what your people did. I find that really hard to believe you'd come here," he said and smiled.

"Oh well, I think that was a long time ago. I can let it go if you can," she said. Joe shrugged. "Yeah okay, ancient history isn't anything to be upset about I guess. But there isn't much to see here anymore, the town is, well, dying I think," Joe said and his mood turned a little sad. "Oh, cheer up Joe man, think about it, you're all still here and it looks good right now, right?" she asked.

"Yeah, I guess," Joe said and Jenny looked around. "Alright, truth is I am working on a book about all these small towns. Is there anything special around here that might be of interest?" she asked and his eyes glazed over a little bit, he shook his head. "Special, uh, no I don't think so," he replied and shrugged. "What you see is what you get around here. Red sand and elves crazy enough to live out here," he replied.

"Anyway. I got to go home now," Joe said, as if his personality shut off and something else took over. Jenny nodded and realized that the block was something about this town. Of course, this had to be a town with a dark secret. There was no way this secret and the case weren't connected. How, she didn't know just yet. This only meant one thing, more digging and more investigation. Jenny looked over to her left and saw Caine hitting on someone else who was clearly disgusted with him already.

"What an idiot," Jenny said and started to make her way towards the bar only to notice that Cornell wasn't there anymore. "Damn it," she said and quickly made her way back outside. He wasn't here either. She took off running to the left and quickly made her way behind the building. Cornell was standing there holding a red mirror in his hand and staring into it. Bright red sparks were starting to fly off of it.

"Cornell, wait," Jenny said and pulled his arm down. "What, why, what's going on?" he asked and glared. "Don't you think it'd be a little suspicious if the Red Mirror shows up after only two new people come to town the same day? Let's wait just a little bit," she said and he shook his head. "Sorry. I just want answers and I hate being blocked," he said and put the mirror back in his pocket.

"Trust me, wait until tomorrow night. This town has a secret and I think it could use a little more Cornell and less Red, at least for now. Everyone is at the bar. One of us needs to go to the church and look around, the other needs to stay here and keep everyone busy," Jenny said.

"Fine, I'll go investigate the creepy church, at night, alone," he replied and she smirked. "Oh, I think you'll be okay," she replied and with that the two of them went their separate ways. Cornell stepped back around the building just in time to see Joe, his target, disappear around a corner. "Next time, Joe," he said, then turned his attention back to the church. It was time to see what was inside that thing.

# Chapter Five

Cornell walked down the path, alone. The cold air was starting to get to him. More to the point, however, it felt like he was being watched. He looked around and didn't see anyone but that didn't matter. There were a hundred different ways of being watched from a distance if you knew how to do it. He decided to keep going, the Loa church wasn't that far from here. He walked up the hill, right up to the front door.

Traditionally, there was always supposed to be someone here. A priest of some kind to represent the everlasting flame of Loa. He knocked on the door. No one showed up. Mere mortals had to sleep, he supposed that was the case this time. He knocked again, this time a little louder just to make sure.

The front door clicked and slowly opened. A woman dressed in the priestess garb was behind the door. "Hello," she said and the voice, this was the one who cast the memory block in the meeting. Not the mayor like he thought. "Hi, I'm Cornell Night-worth. Mystic Force detective. I was wondering if I could have a look around?" he introduced himself with a question.

She narrowed her eyes a little, he wondered if that was on purpose or a response thing. "It's almost midnight, surely, oh never mind come in," she said changing her mind right away and stepped aside. Cornell walked inside, looking around.

"I am Priestess Lexa, what can I do for you?" she asked and he turned around. "I'm going to get right to the point. Six dead people were found in your town. I was wondering if you know anything or anyone told you anything that might help," he said as he turned to look at her.

"As you are well aware, the Covenant of Fire prevents me from telling anything I was told from one of the people who gather here," Lexa replied and Cornell shook his head. "Listen. I'm not asking about affairs, or drug problems, anything like that. I am only interested in finding out why six elves were cut up and dropped in the middle of your town," he said and continued, "I know how people feel about talking to the cops, but they'll spill everything to priests and bartenders," he said and the thought occurred to him that maybe he should have asked the bartender first.

Lexa smiled. "I am well aware of what happened, but I don't know anything. No one around here does. If they did, I am sure they would all be lining up to help. All of the information that I have, well, none of it would interest you. Its all about affairs, petty secrets and addiction," she replied.

Cornell looked around the place. It was old, but well kept. In his mind he pictured an old, broken down place full of dust and cobwebs, but that was just not the case. It wasn't too bad in here. Even the green fire of Loa was lit at the front of the place just behind the podium.

"Well, is there any reason at all you can think of that would attract a psychopath like that? It takes someone of either great insanity or lots of conviction to do things like this and they rarely choose places at random. Insane or not this has to be part of a plan," Cornell said and she just shrugged.

"I was assigned here a few years ago. I give my sermons, do my job, keep the flame lit," she replied, "and I'll move on as we all do in a few years, that's just how it works," Lexa finished and

Cornell knew that was how it worked. He also knew this was a load of lies, at least most of it. Maybe she was protecting the town somehow, if he was he didn't understand it yet.

"Alright, but if you can think of anything else, or you're lying," he said and she spoke up. "Yes, I am aware of the Mystic Force's legendary truth spells," she said with a smile. "Don't worry. Anything I know that's important to the case, you'll know it too. I promise," she said and the wording of that made him curious.

"Again, you might not think a detail is important but if you think of anything, you know where I am," he replied and looked at his watch, it was almost one in the morning. "Thanks, we'll talk again soon," he said and started walking towards the door. "May Loa be with you," she said and he nodded. "Thanks," he replied and walked right back outside.

He walked down the path only a few steps, then the sound of thunder caught his attention in the distance. He turned to look and sure enough, there were flashes of lightning in the distance. Storms like this in the desert were very rare. He pulled the mirror out of his pocket on a hunch and sure enough the thing was glowing a dim red. That meant there was magic being used in that direction. "Mage storm?" he asked himself, wondering what sort of ritual was going on over there to cause one to happen.

It really didn't matter right now. He ignored it and kept walking down the hill, intent to make it back to his room before the sun came up at least. Every side road he came to pulled at his attention, who knows what was down that way and the next. A clue to the mystery could literally be anywhere, but now wasn't the time to look for it.

The bar was closing, the music had been turned off and drunk elves were slowly making their way out. Jenny hadn't had any luck learning anything new. Everyone she asked immediately got that glazed look in their eyes and slowly walked out. Caine was passed out in a corner with an empty bottle of something about ready to fall out of his hand and Jenny thought that he was pretty pathetic. Not wanting to stay around here anymore she quickly made her way out and began to walk to the hotel.

She didn't walk for more than about three minutes. "Hey Pixie," someone screamed out from behind her and she stopped, turned around. "First off, my name's Jenny, second of all, what?" she asked back. There were three men standing there in the dark.

"Get out of our town you mutant snozbucket," the one in the center said and she narrowed her eyes. This was going to get old really fast. "Your town, sure, just tell me who mutilated the elves and threw them in the middle of your town, and I'm as good as gone," she told them the truth. It was clear these three didn't know who did it.

"We said get out," the one on the left screamed and pulled a gun out. "You do realize that pulling a weapon on an officer of the law is punishable up to thirty years on the Black Isle, right?" she asked them, they didn't seem to care.

"There is no law out here. No one will find your body, you'll just be another statistic, another person who disappeared without a trace," the elf in the middle said with a wicked smile, his teeth and eyes reflected the moonlight. "We are the law out here," the one on the right said and the one with the gun raised it to be in line with her head.

It was far from the first time she had a gun pulled on her like this without back up. Being a Pixie came with natural advantages that most races didn't have. Now she was ready to use them. Just before she could, however, another dressed in a green cloak fell out of the sky and stood between her and the weapon.

"What the hell is that?" the one with the gun said and fired. The bullet melted out of the air before it had the chance to hit anything. The figure in green turned to the elves out stretched his hand and all three of them began to melt. Their skin turned to liquid and steam rose from their bodies. The elves tried to run but their bodies fell apart after a short distance, then they disappeared.

"They will not bother you again," the figure said in a deep voice. Jenny hadn't quite seen anything like that before. "Are you Zozo?" she asked straight out. The figure turned away. "Listen, get out of this town, get far away from it," the figure said in the same raspy, deep voice and began to walk away.

"Hey, stop," Jenny said and usually when she said that, the person did as they were told. This time the figure in green took too more steps and faded away into the night. "Damn it," she said and cursed her luck. She almost wanted to investigate the remains of the melted elves in the distance. There was nothing left but piles of clothes and even they were beginning to burn, as if invisible fire consumed them. There was no heat, and no reason to get closer. Jenny turned around and started to run towards the inn as fast as she could go.

Cornell was just approaching the front of the door when Jenny came running up to him. She came to a stop. "What?" he asked. She took a second to catch her breath. "Mr. Green showed up. Melted three elves. I think it's Zozo," she said and Cornell was skeptical at that information.

"Prime suspect. Firewalker leader thought to be dead. Location unknown. I'm not sure if its him or not. He told me to get out of this town, didn't say why or anything like that but that is what happened," she said and continued. "He's not our killer. A cold blooded killer like him doesn't save a cop and warn them to get away," she said and looked into the dark.

Cornell's eyes widened. "Zozo's dead. I killed him and the Firewalkers," Cornell said and Jenny stepped back. "It was before you found out, back in my early days as the Mirror," he said and Jenny looked at him.

"And you never told me?" she asked. "It was on the news wasn't it," Cornell replied quietly. "Yeah, but no one said you actually killed him," she replied. "Well, I thought I did. I never saw a body, just a lot of fire and explosions as I flew away," he replied with a shrug. Jenny shook her head. "Well, I don't know what to tell you, on the list of the of mages that could cast a proxy spell, he was on it," she said, out of ideas and still coming to terms with what she saw.

Cornell sighed in frustration. "If Zozo is here, I'll find him," he said and put his hand on the doorknob. This was just getting stranger by the minute. The monster he knew never would have spared Jenny's life. "Good, I hope so," she replied as he opened the door and she walked inside. The conversation was over the minute they walked back inside the inn.

The two of them made it to their room. Jenny reached in her bag and pulled out a strip of cloth that barely covered the length of her hand and put it on the desk. "I'm going to take a shower before bed," she said and Cornell nodded, lost in thought. "You know, it's a dry year, maybe to conserve water you should, you know, join me?" she asked without thinking. Cornell looked up and pointed at the light above them with a look.

"You're kidding, right. You know its against protocol for that stuff, the force would have us fired," he said, but at the same time was reminding her to think before she spoke. Any leverage the listeners could get against them would turn into blackmail later, he was sure of it. Jenny put her hand over her mouth, eyes wide in shock.

"It was just a test, good to see you stick to the rules so well, be out in a few minutes," she said in a hurry and closed the door. No one had gone into the bathroom while they were gone but she checked all the obvious places for peep holes and other spying devices, she began her nightly rituals.

Cornell sat on the edge of the bed, he couldn't believe Zozo was still alive. It had been almost ten years since anyone mentioned the name to him. The memories came back in a flood and he couldn't help but smile to remember all the dumb mistakes he made that almost got him killed. He had no idea how Zozo survived the experience actually. Dumb luck he supposed.

The minutes passed by like seconds and the bathroom door opened. Steam rolled out and he could smell a hint of lavender on the vapor. A streak of golden light flew out of the steam and to the desk.

"Good Night, Jen," he said and the point of light flashed bright for a second as it slid under the white cloth. He smiled and walked into the bathroom, shut the door. The steamed up mirror, he wiped a streak away to see his own face. He looked away before he might have seen something else looking back at him other than his own reflection.

"You'll get to the bottom of this, don't worry about it tonight," he said and pulled the ornate Red Mirror out of his pocket and looked at it. "We'll have work to do, friend," he said to it and set it on the shelf on the wall.

# Chapter Six

Cornell woke up, the sun wasn't up yet but he was recharged already. He sat up quietly and stared out the window. Could Zozo really be out there, none of this was his style. It didn't make sense. There was a whole lot of nothing around here and if he was teleporting a great distance, well, he could be anywhere.

There was no point in trying to track him. All he could do now was investigate the case in his own way. Cornell sighed and stood up, walked to his clothes and got dressed. He looked towards Jenny, and could see her there, still on the desk out like a light. She didn't need to be awake for this and he picked up his mirror, stepped inside the bathroom and shut the door. "Coroner's tent," he whispered. His mirror lit up with bright red electric sparks, then he was gone.

He appeared in the Coroner's tent, everything was in black and white. No one was here, however. He looked around to make sure, but the place was small. Anyone else here, he would have seen them. Cornell took one step forward and everything faded back into their proper colors. Wasting no more time he walked to the bodies.

The six of them were there on their tables, but nothing had been done with them since they were found. He didn't understand this because this was the only case they were here to work. Processing should have already been well underway by now, if not finished. There was a yellow envelope on the table beside the bodies. Cornell would get to them in a second, he walked to the thing and picked it up.

Opening it up was easy, it wasn't sealed with wax or anything. Unusual that the thing was unmarked as well. It was likely nothing but looking wasn't going to hurt anything if it was. Inside was one thick sheet of paper with writing on it.

Orders are as follows:

Destroy all evidence of attacks in Larenville after informing the detectives on the case that it was Necromancer cult.

Special Operations is on the case from here.

Burn after reading.

That was all it said. No one signed it, however the Blood Seal of the Vanir Royal Family was there at the bottom. Cornell didn't know what was going on, but now time was limited. If Special Operations was on the case, that means this was more than some Necromancer cult at work. Actually, now that the thought about it, why would have a necromancer of any kind have wasted six perfectly good bodies and cut them up. He was astonished that he didn't think of that yesterday and was feeling pretty stupid about it right now.

He put the letter back inside and set it back down where he found it. Then he turned to the bodies. "Alright, let's see what you remember," Cornell said to the dismembered bodies. "Zintero Mosk Loen," he said as he held his right hand out to the first body, a woman. His hand began to glow bright red as said the words.

"And, as I was saying. Never mix Hulian wine with, wait," a spirit of a lady elf wearing thin party clothes appeared talking about something, then realized she was somewhere else. "What is going on?" she asked. "Sorry. My name is Cornell Nightworth,

I'm a detective for the Mystic Force. You were killed, you and your friends. I need to find out who did it," he said.

She tilted her head. "Mystic force, and I'm dead. A ghost," she said and continued. "How is a mystic force detective talking to me. Necromancers aren't allowed on the force last I heard," she replied and he cleared his throat a little. "Uh, top secret experimental stuff. Don't tell anyone," Cornell replied and she wasn't stupid.

"You're a necromancer on the force," she said and her pale green eyes got big. "Okay, you got me, please don't tell anyone. So, who killed you?" he asked, getting right back to the point.

"You're pretty cute for a Necromancer, doing anything later tonight?" she asked and he shook his head. "What, no, you're a ghost. I don't think it would work," Cornell replied and she frowned. "Okay well. This is all I know. We were at a party, pretty high class stuff. The six of us here were having a good time when suddenly we were approached by a particularly handsome young human," she said and smiled.

"What did this human look like, a name maybe?" Cornell asked. She shrugged. "Shorter than you, brown hair, pale skin. I don't know, all the humans look the same to me," she said. "But his name was William, I do remember that. No last name," she said and Cornell knew he couldn't get that lucky.

"He was pretty convincing. Told us about a new club that we should try. It was called The Poison Cup, he said. He sold it pretty well and the night was young, so we went," she said and he narrowed his eyes. "The Poison Cup?" he asked, he thought it seemed like a crazy name for a nightclub.

"Yeah. The place was crazy busy. There were lots of people, loud music and cheap drinks. The place was amazing," she said. "Then the waitress in gold came to our table and offered us all a complimentary drink. Said everyone who came in got one. It was some strange green stuff. It smelled like Ento and it was just a shot. So, we all took one," she said and looked down.

"I suppose I seem pretty dumb to you," she said. Cornell shook his head. "No, what happened to you wasn't your fault. Maybe a little bit for going to a place called the Poison Cup and then drinking something you didn't pay for, but yeah, most of it wasn't your fault," he replied and she laughed a little.

"Looking back on it, it does seem kind of dumb to go to a place called that, but yes. Shortly after that I remember the room spinning. I think we all felt out of it. One by one we started to pass out. Everything went black for me. The next thing I knew I was in Sarjenia. I figured I was dead but, it didn't feel any different," she said and shrugged.

"Thanks, you've told me enough to find out who did this and why. What's your name, anyway?" Cornell asked. "My name is—" she was cut off when someone opened the front door. Cornell didn't want to risk getting caught. "Oeal," he whispered and she faded away, waving as she did with a smile. Cornell stepped back into the black and white just before the Coroner walked around the corner.

"Oh hell," the dwarf said as he moved to the envelope. "I don't want to forget this," he said and picked it up. Dorf looked around, something felt like it was out of place but he didn't see anything obvious, so he went to get the incinerator ready for the bodies. On the way back, he stepped through Cornell and shivered as if he passed through a ghost but kept walking.

Cornell quickly reached through the dimensions and grabbed a severed hand. You could contact a ghost without their remains but it took a lot more effort and If you didn't know their name, it was next to impossible. He was almost sure no one would miss a hand, and even if they did they wouldn't worry too much about it.

He pulled the hand back and quickly teleported back to the bathroom. He was there in a second and now he kind of knew what he had to do next, but also, he knew what was coming their way. He put his hand on the doorknob, it opened before he could do it. "Oh, I didn't think anyone was in, wait, why do you have a hand?" she asked him as she saw it. Jenny was confused, but not surprised at the sight.

"Everyone has hands, now hurry up, we need to go out to get something to eat," Cornell said, once again pointing up, whoever was listening was still there. Jenny shook her head, that was the second time she forgot. "Yeah, I'll be out in a few minutes," she said and the two of them switched places.

Cornell quickly put the severed hand in his bag and started to pack up what little things there was to pack. He sat down on the edge of the bed and waited. The wait was not a long one. Jenny came back out and was ready to go. "Just let me get my bed and we can get out of here," she said and walked to the desk, picked up the tiny cloth and she stuffed it in her pocket.

He stood up and nodded, it was time to go. The two of them left in a hurry and made it into the pre-dawn morning hours. "I have news," he said and continued, "We're going to be off the case. Special Operations is going to take over. The order comes from the Royals, I don't know why," he said. She already knew how he knew.

"I suppose the hand in your bag is going to be the last of the evidence we have the case ever happened," she said. He nodded. "Without it, its like the six of them never existed. That's why the missing persons report wasn't found, they intercepted it," he said and she stopped. "What are we going to do? If they order us to stop, we kind of have to," she said, frustrated at the turn of events.

"We'll keep on the case, but on our own time. Until we get the official order we keep working as if nothing has changed. I'll talk to the bartender, you track down that guy you were talking to who disappeared at the bar," he said.

"Screw that, I want to know why desk girl put a listening device in our room," she replied, tired of messing around when time was so limited. "Fine, lets ask her right now," Cornell said and turned right back around and started walking back towards the inn. Jenny was shocked he agreed so easily and turned with him.

As they walked in, she was behind the desk acting normal. "Checking out?" she asked with that same smile as ever.

"Maybe. So, why were you in our room after we left and put a listening device in the light overhead," Jenny asked and leaned up against the desk. The smile disappeared at once. "I, uh, I have no–"Cornell cut her off. "Stop, we have you recorded with an image tracer. Don't lie, don't screw with us. Who put you up to it?" he asked, staring straight into her green eyes.

She shook her head. "I'm sorry. I was just doing what I was told. Someone approached me with a thick roll of cash and the machine. "This job only pays so much, I couldn't say no," she said and looked away. "And?" Jenny asked again.

The woman shook her head. "I can't say who it was. I'll be exiled. I have no where to go," she said and started to break down. Cornell knew that exile was a harsh punishment for the desert towns like this. It was a death sentence most of the time to betray the local authorities.

"I have you covered. Just tell me who it was and you'll be fine. I promise," Cornell said and her eyes darted around, looking for anyone who might be listening. "Okay, fine. It was Elrond May. The Mayor's assistant," she said in a barely audible whisper. Cornell rolled his eyes.

"How arrogant does this person think they are, couldn't they have hired a random person to do it to make the money drop?" Jenny asked. "Well it is a small town, I'm sure the mayor thought no one else could be trusted," Cornell said.

"Damn it what about me, how are you going to protect me," she complained almost too loudly. "Trust me. I have you covered," Cornell said as he made his way back to the room to get the device. "We have a plan, and worst case situation and they exile you anyway, we can set you up in the city somewhere.

You're good," Jenny replied and fully intended to help if she needed to. However, Jenny had no idea what Cornell's plan really was.

It wasn't a long wait until Cornell returned holding the broken bug in his hand. "Thanks," he replied and started to leave. Jenny followed him. The woman behind the desk waited, nervously, now more than ever. "The mayor lives in the big green house at the end of the road, you can't miss it," she blurted out as they were walking away.

"Thanks," Cornell said as they walked out and the door shut behind them.

# Chapter Seven

The Mayor of Larenville rested behind her work desk. Her hand grasping on to a pen, nervously. "What are we going to do, they know, that snozbucket had to have betrayed us," Elrond said and she glared at him. "What, didn't you pay her enough money. Maybe you are to blame for this disaster," she replied in a near hiss. The broken bug going offline was a good enough sign that they had been discovered, and they were on their way here.

"I should fire you," she said again as the front door opened. "Hi, I'm Mystic Force Detective, Cornell Nightworth, and I have some questions," he said as he walked inside, Jenny right beside him. "You can't just come in here like this, there are protocols and procedures. This is uncalled for," she replied and stood up.

Cornell slammed the listening device on the desk. "Talk," he said in a deeper, angrier voice. Elrond and the Mayor looked at it. "No idea what that thing is I mean—" Cornell cut her off with a gaze filled with unnatural anger. "My own listening coin picked up on it the second we came back into the room. Did you enjoy listening to our conversations?" he asked her but never broke eye contact.

Jenny picked up the bug and Cornell put his hand on the edge of the desk and slid it across the floor with one arm. The thing must have weighed four hundred pounds being made out of some kind of thick wood. It moved with a soft groan as it slid across the floor. Elrond and the Mayor both took a step back.

"Please, start talking. You tried to spy on an officer of the law and that gives me every right to arrest you on the spot, or worse if I feel like it," Cornell said and the Mayor sat back down in her chair. "Alright, we spied on you, but its not what you think," she said and Jenny shrugged.

"We thought you were here to look for it," the Mayor said and Cornell grunted in frustration, time was running out and here she was, playing games. "Get on with it," he said and she looked away. "It's the pixie, the minute we saw her we knew it had to be found. We needed to be sure you weren't here for it," she said and looked away.

"What in the hell are you people talking about, here for what?" Jenny asked, getting frustrated with all of this nonsense.

"The fort, the, the place under the sand," Elrond finally said and continued. "It goes back to the war, the last war," he finished. Jenny was annoyed, back to this again. Cornell shrugged, the war didn't mean anything to him. "Listen, all we are here for was the six bodies. That's it. We didn't know about your little secret and we still don't care," Cornell said and it was true.

"Little secret, if you knew, if you even had a speck of what was out there you would be just as paranoid as we were, especially beside that, that thing you call a partner," the Mayor said. Jenny tilted her head and didn't understand what was going on. "Alright. I've had just about enough of that nonsense. Call her anything other than her name and I'll make you eat your teeth," Cornell said, and rethought it in a second. "No, I think I'll make you eat his," he said and pointed to the assistant.

The both of them shifted nervously and Jenny just smiled the whole time.

"Fine, Elrond. I guess you might as well show them," she said and the assistant looked at her. "And break the tradition, no I think I'd rather eat my own teeth than let a Pixie know anything," he replied and Cornell was about to act when the phone on his belt began to buzz. He picked it up but knew what was on the other end.

"Hello," he said and waited a few seconds. "Yes, I understand," he replied and hung up. "Come on, let's go," Cornell said, frustrated and began to walk out.

"I'll have your badges for this, you hear me. You're going to be off the force before you get home," the mayor yelled as they walked away, the two of them ignored it as the walked out the door and closed it behind them.

"Don't worry about it. They'll need to explain to high command about all of their so called secrets and I don't think they want to do that. But, as you might have guessed, we're off the case," Cornell said and looked down the road. Never before has such a little town caused him so many headaches and dead ends.

"So, Special ops are going to take over. We must have stumbled on to something huge," Jenny said and Cornell smiled. "Don't worry. We're not done. I'll just have to take a different approach to all of this," he replied as they walked down the road.

"Or we could just go back home and pretend that none of this ever happened," she suggested and he shook his head. "If Zozo is involved, I at least need to look into it," he replied. "Yeah, I guess there isn't much of a choice, even though there totally is," she said, with a little annoyance in her voice and just about then a black helicopter flew overhead, followed by another one.

"Well, that didn't take long," Jenny said as the helicopters landed in middle of town where the bodies were found. Men dressed in black uniforms jumped out, it was impossible to know what race they were or anything. That was just how Special Ops worked, completely in secret.

A trio of the men in black met the detectives half way to the choppers. "I believe you've been informed. Your ride home is the helicopter with the red mark on thc tail. Get on it asap. Oh, if you have any evidence about this case on you, please hand it over," the man in the middle said.

Cornell shrugged. "There wasn't any evidence to collect, we've barely been here a day," he replied. "Very well, thank you, but your services are no longer required," the man said, then the three of them walked around the pair. "Not the friendliest bunch, are they?" Jenny asked. "No, but it's just the job. Come on, let's get out of here," Cornell said and kept walking, keeping his bag close to his side.

The trip to the flying machine only took a few minutes. Cornell allowed Jenny to get inside first then he followed, shutting the sliding door behind him. Just after the two of them got settled in, the helicopter took off. Jenny looked down at the town with a secret she could only feel as if they were mere minutes away from knowing, yet now they might never know it. Nothing was worse than that. Cornell, on the other hand, had no intention of staying in the dark about it for very long.

"Don't worry," he said to Jenny, and she hated it when he said stuff like that. It only meant one thing. The one thing that could get them both sent to prison. "Damn it," she said, but kept looking out the window as Larenville disappeared behind them in a hurry.

The trip on the machine didn't take more than a couple of hours before they were at a Mystic Force outpost. It landed and Cornell opened the door and got out. They walked away from the windy, noisy machine and inside the outpost. It wasn't long before someone was there to greet them, a middle aged human with graying hair and tired blue eyes, a tad bit overweight.

There on his gray shirt the name tag Anton Rizzy in small white letters was pinned there, tilted and looked just as tired as he was. "Sorry for that, guys. We honestly don't know what happened. We got a call from the talking heads and the case wasn't ours anymore," Anton said to them.

Jenny shrugged. "It happens all the time, Rizzy," she replied with a half smile. "It still doesn't make it right, Commander," Cornell replied, almost sad about the situation as a whole.

"Well, we have a couple of rooms ready for you down the hall. It'll be a couple of days before we get you back home, you know how the desert transports are," Anton said and shrugged. "So, enjoy the time off I guess. There will be plenty to do back in the city," Anton said with a sigh as he turned and walked away to focus on the rest of his duties.

"I'll see you in a while," Cornell said and she looked at him. "I think you can let this one go, it's not worth it. Let the Operation people take care of it this time," she said and he rolled his eyes. "I can't and you know it. If Zozo really is involved I need to find out why, how, all the usual questions," he replied in a whisper.

"Damn it," she said and looked away. "If you get caught, don't drag me down with you," she added and he smiled. "You got it," he replied and with that, she started to walk to her room down the hall. He sighed and followed her.

# Chapter Eight

Cornell sat in his room on the bed. This one was leagues better than the one in Larenville. Even though he could have sworn someone asked him if the case was related to some kind of Unicorn attack but none of the news channels were even reporting on something remotely close to that. He supposed it was nothing after all, or some kind of an attempt to get information out of him. It didn't make much sense.

He looked out the window and saw that the sun was starting to go down, it wouldn't be long now before he could get to work. But first he was going to get something to eat. He turned off the television and made his way to the cafeteria. It wasn't a very long trip.

There were a few others here, people like him, just here waiting to go to a case or go home he supposed, but really didn't care. He didn't know any of them and didn't care to start to know them. He walked to a table and sat down alone. The holographic menu popped up in front of him and he pressed his selection, there were only three things to pick from.

"How's it going," someone said and sat down across from him. Cornell's menu disappeared as he looked up. "Rigin, it's fine. What are you doing out all the way out here?" he asked, honestly curious. The man sighed. "A couple of beheaded corpses were found outside some dirt town way out next to the Scorched wall," he replied and Cornell laughed.

"What, are those stupid immortals at it again?" Cornell said and Rigin's arm sparked a little. Cornell looked away. "The dust is hell on my cybernetics," he said and continued. "Yeah, I think they are doing their little game again, the whole head rolling thing is tad extreme. It turned out be a newbie anyway," he said and smiled.

"Yeah, six dismembered elves in Larenville. Clean cuts, professional. Jen and I were making some progress when Special Ops took the case," he said with a shrug. "I know how that is, sucks when they swoop in and take all the fun out of the job," Rigin replied. "Yeah, and it's always a damn secret too. I wonder what kind of thing that town has to hide that would interest them," Cornell wondered. "Not for us to know," Rigin replied and his metal arm sparked again.

"Damn it, I need to get this thing to the shop," he said and Cornell nodded. "" I think the repair place is still open if you hurry. It could be a long night if that thing keeps acting up," Cornell said and Rigin stood up. "Yeah anyway, good seeing you again, say hi to Jen for me," he said and walked away.

Seconds later his food appeared out of his table and he looked at it. It was not impressive, a thin meat sandwich and a small white foil bag of generic chips. He didn't want to know what kind of meat it was. A plastic glass of water that was barely enough to wash anything down with. He was not impressed with any of it.

It only took a few minutes to eat it. It didn't taste like much of anything but at least he was no longer hungry. He looked out the big window that provided the natural light in the day. The sun was deep red as it was falling out of the sky. He lost his thoughts as he focused on the red light for a few minutes.

Someone walked between him and the light, snapping him out of the zone. He shook his head and stood up. Pressing the small red button on the table beside him, the tray and the remains of food on it, disappeared. He quickly started to make his way back to the room.

When he got there, Jenny was waiting for him. "Are you really, seriously going to go back there?" she asked, arms crossed. "You know I have to," he replied and she rolled her eyes. "The world was just fine with out you, it will be fine if you just sleep here tonight," she said to him. He considered it for a few seconds.

"You know that if Zozo is involved, I have to go see what he's up to. Special Operations may be walking into some kind of trap and that's the best case scenario here," Cornell said and looked towards the darkening sky. "Yeah, I know," she replied and looked in the same direction. "Just, you know," she said and he smiled. "Yeah, I know, don't worry about it, now stand back," he replied, she stepped back, but was never sure why. The sparks never hurt.

Without a second thought he pulled the old red mirror out of his pocket and opened it. All at once it felt like a thousand red sparks flew through the room and covered his body at once, but in a flash, he was gone. "Good luck," she said and sat down on the bed. With any luck, no one would come looking for him any time soon.

Cornell appeared in Larenville on the top of the Arrow and Quiver out of a red mist that disappeared quickly. He was dressed in his red armored suit. He crouched down and looked over the street. The place was dead but this being the bar, there should have been activity. However, right now there was nothing. It was easy to see why in just few seconds.

A black car slowly drove down the street coming right at him with its headlights off. Special operations were still here and they had locked the town under a curfew. It only complicated things a little more, but it wasn't anything he didn't expect. First, he had a mayor to talk to. He lifted himself into the darkening sky and shot through the desert air without a sound. The car on the road never saw him.

Cornell flew through the air, within seconds the green house the mayor lived in was in view, and so were the two guards posted by the front door. He landed quietly on the house across the way. He narrowed his eyes and all of the guards inside began to glow bright yellow, however, the only one who was worth talking to was Elrond, the Mayor was not here. Cornell supposed he would have to do for now. There were only two choices left to make. The direct approach or to go through the window.

He was in something of a hurry, so he decided the window was the best approach. Elrond was sitting on a chair. The guard was sitting in another chair across from him. He sailed over the heads of the ones standing out front, they never even bothered to look up. In seconds he was floating outside the second story window. He tapped on it lightly three times.

Inside, the guard, bored with his duty to watch this nobody jumped at the taps on the glass. "What?" he asked and Elrond just shrugged. "Don't look at me. I'm over here," Elrond said, but he was just as nervous as the guard. He didn't move away from the window out of fear of being shot on accident or in a. The guard picked up his radio. "This is position three, I have a disturbance outside the second floor window. Could you investigate?" he said and let the button go.

"We're on it, stand by," a voice replied. Cornell looked to the two at the front, they both were moving in his direction. "Both of them. My lucky day," he said to himself as he pulled himself to the roof and floated back to the front. As soon as the front door was clear he landed on the ground, walked to the front door. The door was locked but he twisted the knob until the lock inside the door snapped. He pushed the door open and shut it behind him, hoping no one would notice the damage.

"Yeah, it must be the wind or a bird. There isn't anything up there. This place is dead as hell," the guard said into his radio with a laugh. The man in the room with Elrond didn't feel much better, he knew something was up, it had to be.

The two of them made their way back to their posts. Elrond shrugged again. "Don't look at me, I don't know anything, even now," he said. The guard narrowed his eyes.

It was about then the door to the room opened and a man dressed all in red, sleek armor rushed in and slammed his fist into the guards' face before he had time to do anything. Before he could fall to the floor and make any noise, he was caught and set gently on the floor. "We need to talk," he said as he turned to look at Elrond.

# Chapter Nine

"Oh, Loa, please don't hurt me. I think I know who you are," Elrond said just before he tried to scream. Cornell closed the distance and put his hand over the mouth. "Quiet, we're going for a quick ride, too," he said. He quietly opened the window without a sound with his left hand. Cornell grabbed him with the other hand and together they flew into the star filled sky.

"Talk," he said in his altered voice. "I don't know anything," Elrond replied as the two of them flew higher into the cold air. "Really. I could have sworn they were guarding you to prevent someone like me from getting a hold of you, now talk," Cornell said to him again. "If you don't talk. I'm dropping you," he finished. Elrond looked at the steadily shrinking desert under him.

"Damn it, fine," he said, terrified. "They're here for him, part of him. The man in green. I don't know who that was. But they were here for him," Elrond said and Cornell rolled his eyes under his helmet.

"Who, why, details," Cornell demanded, he wasn't in the mood to waste time. "The heart of the last Vampire King. You know. The last war we had. Larenville wasn't always a low down nothing dirt town. A vampire stronghold was here. At the end of the war, the King was on the run. The allied forces, they killed him here," Elrond said all at once and Cornell stopped in midair.

"What, no, that's not how history went. Everyone knows the last vampire king was killed at the Battle of Green Cliff, you're not making any sense sand lizard," Cornell said, angry with the lies. "No, I'm serious. Me, almost everyone in Larenville is a descendant of the dismemberment. It's a secret, a well kept one for the past century but someone knows. What's left of the fort is over there, the spires, they look like rock formations but get closer," Elrond said and Cornell was pretty sure he was being taken for a ride right now.

He flew towards the rock formation in the distance and closed it in just a few minutes. Sure, enough there were three black cars there outside and an open tunnel leading into the unknown. The guy was right after all. "Here's what I'm going to do. I'm going to drop you off here and you walk back to town. If anyone asks, make up a good story that doesn't involve med," Cornell said and as a red aura formed around Elrond.

"Drop?" he asked, worried. "Don't worry, the impact shield is good for one, you might not even break anything," he said and dropped Elrond without a second thought. Elrond struggled in vain to try and grab on to anything as he dropped through the air, helplessly. It was only about ten seconds but he hit the ground with a thud. His impact spell took all the force and faded away when he hit the dirt. Now he was at least a mile from town and in the dark. "Damn it," he said to himself as he looked around, hoping he didn't run into anything horrible on the walk back home.

Cornell didn't see anyone waiting at the gates so he flew down and landed in front of the stone gate with the tunnel leading into the ground. He wondered if there really was something to that story, likely there was. He took a deep breath, then he walked into the dark to see what he could.

Despite being so dark he could see everything. The tunnel was a basic square leading steadily down into the earth. It was all quiet for the first few minutes, then he could hear voices coming from the other end, and bright yellow sparks.

"Are you sure they got the door open, if they did, why did they close it behind them?" one man said. "Who knows, just keep trying to cut through this stupid thing and we'll figure it out later," another replied and the sparks continued.

Cornell stopped a few feet behind the dark and he saw a mage holding his arm up. A ray of light was burning against a strange black door. There were symbols on it. Necromancy symbols. These idiots were doing their best to break open a mystically sealed door with necromancy. "Hey, you guys are never going to break through that door without a necromancer. You better give up now," Cornell said to them.

The two special operations agents stopped what they were doing and turned around. "Oh, Taro, it's the Red Mirror, what's he doing here," the one on the left said and backed off. "I thought he was a myth," the other said and his hand began to glow bright yellow.

"Gentlemen, you have two choices. You're not the bad guys here so you can either work with me, or leave," Cornell said to them. The two agents looked at one another. "We need to get through this door, can you do it?" the one on the left asked him and Cornell shrugged. "I can try, but if we are working together, names, I'll need yours," he replied.

"I'm Rais, the mage here is Ghul," Rais replied and they both took off their helmets. Cornell had no idea why Rais was a halfling, but a mix of what, Cornell wasn't sure Ghul was an orc, pure blooded for sure. "Alright, what's behind that door that is so special?" he asked and Ghul shook his head he didn't want to say.

"Vampire King's heart. I can't tell you too much, state secrets. But we need to verify its still there. The dead bodies in this town was a message," Rais replied and Cornell knew all of that, at least the information was verified now.

He walked forward and the two got out of his way. "Magic is just like math, once a formula or spell is made, it doesn't change. This is a dual barrier," he said and walked to the side. "Was the stone tunnel open when you got here, or did you open it?" Cornell asked. "It was already open," Ghul said and continued, "we thought it was strange, but then it could have always been like this," he replied.

Cornell shook his head. "Use your brains, if this place was open for that long there'd be sand everywhere, this whole tunnel would be filled with it. This was opened by someone very recently," he said and walked to the strange symbols. "Six very full blood locks. Makes sense they would use these. Vampires don't have blood of their own," Cornell was mostly talking to himself. There were three deep red cylinders on both sides of the vault door.

"It wasn't normal blood. It had to be willing, a sacrifice. Who ever did this was able to get what they needed with no resistance," Ghul replied and Cornell stopped what he was doing he knew that but he was hoping they didn't. "Anything else you'd like to share before I figure this thing out so we can all go home?" he asked. Neither of them had anything to say as they took a step back.

"Are your really sure you want this thing open. I mean, who ever did this couldn't break the magic seals. Chances are they're waiting for someone to open it. Then they can swoop in and take what they want," Cornell replied.

"Mr. Mirror, or is it just Red. We have the whole town locked down. State of the art surveillance cameras and wards around here. No one is getting in," Rais said with pride. Cornell rolled his eyes. "Red is fine, and well, I got in here pretty easily. If I could do it, someone else could too," he replied, but didn't bother looking back at them.

"So, are you really sure this needs to be done?" he asked again. "Orders from the top," Rais replied and Cornell sighed. "Good, find yourself a high level necromancer and get it done," Cornell replied, turned and started to walk away.

"You're a citizen of the Southern Kingdom. We have the same authority as the King himself in this situation. I am ordering you to open this vault if you are able to do it," Rais said and his tone changed, even if it was a bit shaky now. Cornell stopped in his tracks. "Really," he said and turned around.

"Well, if you insist. However, you need to put your helmets on. This spell is going, well, it can be a little bit bright. Old spells, when they break, they tend to flash a little bit. Your eyes might burn for a few days If you don't protect them," Cornell said and waited. "I'm not doing it until you do what I tell you," Cornell said and they put their helmets on.

"Good, now stand back. This could get messy," he said to them and walked forward. Cornell shook his head and stared at the oddly marked vault door. He raised his hands. "Habuski," he said quietly but nothing happened.

"I don't understand that magic word, what does it do?" Ghul asked as he took a step closer. "Habuski," Cornell yelled, lunged in Ghul's direction and grabbed him by the collar of his jacket in one fluid motion. Then he spun around, taking the agent with him and threw him into his partner. Rais turned to look and only had enough time to put his hands up.

The two agents collided together and slammed into the stone wall. "Good thing you had your helmets on," he said with a smile they'd never see. He knew they were both alive. Cornell was going to empty the blood locks when a gunshot rang out. The bullet struck his left shoulder, then the hot metal deflected into the opposite wall.

"As I live and breathe, it's Mr. Mirror himself," a voice said and he turned around. It wasn't anyone he knew. She stood there, a human vampire stood there with two mindless troll thralls at her side. They barely fit through the entrance. "Yeah, I was just about to drag these two out of here, seal the entrance and never come back here again. I'm glad to see that you've brought some people to help," he replied.

She smirked, but didn't lower her weapon. "I'm here for the item behind the door. I heard what you told the scrubs here. You can open that door," she said and Cornell shook his head. "What makes you think you're going to have better luck than the agents here or I didn't just lie about the whole thing?" he asked right back.

"Well, you can either do it nicely, or I can have my two pals here start beating you to death. Or I can just kill the agents here and make you watch. The word is you have something of a soft spot for people," she replied in a hiss.

"Oh yes, people sure, but I barely consider the agents here people. Do you know how many times they've gotten messed up in things they didn't need to and just get in the way?" he asked and she was tired of the conversation. With the smallest flash of her pure red eyes, the troll bodyguards began to lumber in his direction. "Alright," he said to himself. They would do this the hard way. He'd faced a few vampires in the past, tough enemies but not unbeatable.

Cornell prepared to fight the brutish bodyguards when suddenly her deep, red eyes began to burn blue. "Oh hell," he said as she flashed forward. To any normal being, this was usually a death sentence. He watched as she flew through the air, he just barely able to react. Cornell grabbed her wrists as the fingernails turned into claws stopped mere inches from his helmet. "What does an Elder Vampire have to do with this?" he asked as he threw her. She landed on all fours, vertical against the wall. "I want what anyone like me wants you idiot, power," she replied as she jumped off the wall and landed on her feet.

"Don't you have enough?" Cornell asked, he should have known right away this was no ordinary vampire, red eyes weren't strong enough to create thralls like this. He cursed his stupidity but focused on the now. The two large, pale green trolls lunged at him. He leapt into the air, over their heads. At the same time put one hand on the backs of their head each and forced them both face first into the old, black stone wall.

He knew this wasn't going to slow them down at all. They were too slow to be a threat anyway, they were here for the agents. He jumped forward the vampire who bared her dead white, and long fangs. She copied his movements and was just a fraction of a second faster. Her left fist and the incredible power behind it connected. Cornell was thrown to the side and hit the wall. Even with the magical armor, he felt that. It wasn't too often he was hurt.

"You are outmatched, human, or whatever you are. Give up now and do what I ask, or the agents will be torn to pieces," she said and pointed. Cornell looked and the brutes had a hold of them. In the troll's hands, they looked just like toys from here. "Damn it," he said to himself and took a step back. The last thing he needed was two dead agents to be blamed for.

"Again, you must be at least a thousand years old. You're an elder vampire. Why would you want to dredge up the past, just keep looking towards the future?" he asked again, trying to appeal to something close to common sense.

"What future, in a thousand years I've seen my people go from the top of the food chain to being forced to live in the Morglands, restricted in every single way you can imagine. We are only seen as parasites, and you talk about a future. We don't have a future. Our leader is a puppet controlled by all the royal strings of all the so called royal families. I looked for a century for this place. This, red sand filled hell. The last person who is going to get in my way is someone who wears a, albeit powerful, mage artifact and acts like a superhero with it," she said, Cornell supposed that it was easy to talk that much when you didn't need to breathe.

"This will not go how you think," Cornell said and continued. "I have your word, the agents live if I do this, attempt this?" he asked and she tilted her head. "No, but you have five seconds to get started then they are dead for sure," she replied. "Fine, I'll do it," he said and turned to face the vault door. The last thing you ever wanted to do was turn your back on a vampire, but he had no choice if he wanted to.

The method of opening the lock was easy, but only a high leveled Necromancer could do it. Cornell had rejected the ways of his people, but the knowledge had come in handy many times before now. "Azralynn Delti Manix Arwulf," he said and pointed his hands at the wall. Anyone could say the words, that was easy. The power needed within, the level of focus was something entirely different. Dark green bolts of energy flew from his hands, they hit the vault door and the power flowed through the crevasses and bends of the ornately carved door.

For a few seconds there was nothing, then the thing clicked several times. With a groan of resistance, the century old dust shook from the edges and the door slid into the ground slowly. "Let them go, now," Cornell said the second it was lowered. She smiled and nodded to her thralls, they dropped the agents to the ground and she walked forward.

Cornell walked into the chamber as well. It was black in here. In the center of the room there was an iron box. It was barely bigger than a package one might get in the mail. "So, this is the prize they locked away?" Cornell asked, he wasn't that impressed and he was sure that it wasn't worth the lives of six innocent people.

She walked to it, but then stopped. "It looks like they didn't want any vampire crossing the threshold," Cornell said and almost smiled. He did his part and now the truce was over. He formed a black bone stake in his left hand as quietly as he could. "No cleric's ward is going to stop me," she said and motioned for her trolls to come pick the package up.

With one swift motion he wrapped his right hand around her neck and thrust the long spike through her back, and her dead heart. She only had time to scream for a second before flesh turned to ash and her clothes fell against her bleached bones. Cornell knew his time was limited, the magical spike wouldn't last long. He carefully laid the skeleton down on the floor.

Wasting no time, he rushed to the metal box and picked it up it was heavier than it looked. Not being undead had its advantages. The cleric's ward broke with ease. The two thralls were screaming in pain as their mind control immediately began to break. He flew towards the exit. The agents were still passed out on the ground. "Come with me, idiots," he said and without thinking casted a red light around their bodies. The two of them were lifted off the ground and dragged in tow as he flew out.

Cornell expected something to be waiting for him, but there was nothing but the night and the agent's cars. He was sure she wouldn't have anything to do with them. He got them outside and put them behind their cars. Now at least it would look like the vampire got them first instead of him having anything to do with it if they ended up dead.

Cornell and the package took off into the night sky burning like a red comet as he flew, then he disappeared among the stars.

# Chapter Ten

Cornell reappeared in his room in a red flash. Then he collapsed onto the floor straight to his knees, out of breath and energy. He pushed the metal box away from him and his red armor disappeared. "Oh, Taro, what in the hell happened to you?" Jenny asked as she was startled and jumped off the bed.

"Water," Cornell said still out of breath, everything inside him hurt and his skin felt like it was going to burn at any minute. Jenny rushed to the sink, picked up a small plastic glass and filled it up with water. Brought it to him. He took it and drank the whole thing in one shot. "Thanks," he said, barely feeling better. "What's in the box?" Jenny asked as she walked to it. "Don't know, don't open it. It's bad news whatever it is," he replied, pulling himself to the bed and sitting on the edge of it. "I had to open the necro vault. An elder vampire was waiting for the agents to do it. I never should have gone there," he said and shook his head. "I opened the damn thing for her," he finished.

"Wait, back up," Jenny said and continued, "you did what now," she said again. "I opened the vault, inside that box is the heart of the old vampire King. The one that lead the last war. They want to bring him back, he's not really dead," Cornell said and his eyes widened. "I only managed to get away by staking her with a black bone, that will fade, if it hasn't by now," he said in a panic and looked at the box.

"I'm sure something like that can be tracked. We can't stay here. That vampire will chase it where ever it goes. Not safe here. We need to move," he said and tried to get up but something in his back pulled. All the energy it took to do the necromancy had worn him out. Jenny looked at the clock. "The sun comes up soon, no way a vampire makes her way here before it shows up. We have a little time," she replied, trying to be hopeful.

"Elder vampires have a pretty good sunlight resistance. I don't think its going to help us much," he replied. Jenny didn't know what to say. "Well, we're in a Mystic force outpost and it may not have much, but it's armed to the teeth, we'll be fine for the day at least," Jenny tried to be optimistic about the situation, she didn't know how safe anyone was.

She glanced at the metal box on the floor and found it hard to believe something so small could be the cause of so much trouble. She slid the box under the bed with her foot. "Get some sleep, okay," she said and he groaned as he fell back on to the bed and pulled himself to the pillows. He began to feel cold and started to shiver. Jenny folded the blanket over him as he passed out.

She sat in a chair and faced the window with her gun on her desk beside her. It wouldn't do her a bit of good, but it made her feel better. She stared into the dark desert, scanning for any sign of movement, no matter how slight.

Cornell stood on a desolate plain. The ground was cracked for as far as he could see. He spun around only to see more of the same. He knew this was a dream, it was always the same when he used too much necromantic power. Then the battle horn sounded, a warrior rushed passed him. An ogre dressed in red armor. Then an Orc, a giant's footsteps thundered, a warrior that blocked out the sun. Hundreds rushed past him.

"The alliance," he said as he saw a flag bearing the old colors he recognized from school. Cornell knew that this was a vision of the past on some level. He turned his head at another, less pleasant sound to hear. A grinding of bone and steel. Nothing but a sickly green cloud was swallowing everything that was running into it. The top of the cloud was shaped like a man with white eyes, approaching them without any hint of slowing down.

"Tough people make for soft times. Soft times eventually lead to soft people. Soft people make tough times, and the cycle continues like that," a voice said to him and everything stopped. He turned to look. A woman was standing there in a bright orange dress that looked more like fire.

"This is not the past, this is a possible future that is yet to come," she said and Cornell took a step back. "Who are you?" he asked and she smirked. "My name is Loa, I am, well come on necromancer, you know who I am," she said and he did at once. Also, he felt the impressive need to bow or something in respect.

"Don't bother, I watched your courage, or stupid, act in the vault. You staked that vampire with no hesitation," she said with a smile. "I think it was more stupid than anything. She'll never stop hunting me down after that, I wish I had something more than a magical construct to hit her with," he replied and she nodded. "I suppose so," she said and continued. "Xy won't mind if this takes place but the rest of us kind of like the world the way it is," she said.

"Since you wield the artifact of Osan, the mirror, and it has chosen you. I too have chosen you as my champion. You've proven yourself tonight," she said and Cornell took a step back. He didn't know who or what an Osan was but to be a chosen one, that wasn't really his thing. "Me, I hate to tell you this but I am not very good at the whole champion thing," he replied.

Her eyes blazed with purple and blue fire. "Are you saying no?" she asked him and he quickly changed his mind. "No, I mean, what can I do?" he asked and she smiled. "It's simple, keep the vampire king from being reformed. I don't care how you do it. Take it to my temple. The main one, only there can the heart be destroyed," she said casually.

"Why don't you just do it, right now?" he asked, getting to the point. "I would, but I would risk pissing off Ventrix and Xy. They kind of want the vampires to rise up. They won't help it happen, but if they knew I helped stopped it, well, you know how families and their pets can get," she replied to him in that same flat tone.

"Where is your temple?" Cornell asked, he realized the Gods hadn't been truly worshipped in ages and the revival was still underway since the blade incident. "It's in the desert, Zozo knows where it is. Find him," she said and his eyes went wide. "Oh, come on, I hate that guy," he replied and she just kept smiling. "Funny how that works," she replied. "Can I kill him this time when we're done?" he asked. She shrugged.

"What about Arket, the cosmic flame sword. I know it isn't found. Do you think we could get her help, could you find it?" Cornell asked. Loa shook her head. "That woman doesn't listen to anyone, least of all me, but I can ask. I don't think you'll need her. I mean that might take all the fun out this mission, too," she replied with a slight laugh. He was going to say something else.

Then everything went black and he felt two cold bone fangs dig into his neck. Cornell woke up in a start. His right hand went to his neck but he was fine. The sun was streaming in and all was quiet. His left arm was numb because he was laying on it so he rolled over the best he could. Jenny was passed out in the chair, looking out to the desert.

He was just glad to see the sun and her again but the words in his dream did not leave him. They echoed in his head. "Damn it, I hate quests," he said to himself again in frustration as he knew that his life was about to get a lot more complicated than he liked. The only question now was how many people did he want to get involved. How many more lives did he want to risk losing before this came to an end.

Despite the sun streaming through the window he didn't feel very warm. Right now, he needed to get something to eat. With a little strain he managed to get to the edge of the bed and sit up. Jenny was still sleeping and waking her up felt like the wrong thing to do. He almost wanted to reach under the bed, pull that metal box out and open it up. To see the heart of one of the worst things this world had ever known. Maybe throw it in a garbage disposal and try to blend it to pieces. He also figured if they could have destroyed it like that, they would have done it a hundred years ago, too.

Cornell shook the thoughts from his mind and stood up slowly. It was only then he realized that the Red Mirror was still in his left hand. He pried his stiff fingers off the thing and put it in his pocket, the thing changed shape and size to fit perfectly as it always had before. He took one last look at Jenny, then quietly left the room. He just hoped that no one would notice he was in the same clothes that he was in yesterday and shut the door behind him.

# Chapter Eleven

Cornell made it as far as the mess hall when he noticed something had changed. Special Operations agents were standing outside of the door, trying to look as menacing as possible in their black suits. He quickly turned to not to get their attention, but he wondered what they were doing here. He knew there was no way to track the mirror, and, oh, it hit him then.

This was the closest outpost to Larenville. It must have been routine. Just like everything else that was predictable, there was going to be a search of this place. The agents were going to find the heart, and in turn find him. Cornell cursed his bad luck when he decided to not wipe their memories but he was in a hurry.

He took his phone out of the other pocket and quickly sent Jenny a text in a few seconds, then hoped she'd wake up soon enough to get it. "Oh, the old man finally learned how to text?" a voice asked from behind and he turned around. It was Rigin. "Just texting mom, telling her I'm going to be coming home soon," he replied and turned around, putting his phone away at the same time.

"What's with the suits?" Cornell asked. Rigin just shrugged a little. "Something went down in the desert last night. They've been in Rizzy's office for a half hour now with those goons standing out there," he replied, not being very helpful. "Some detective you turned out to be," Cornell replied with a smile.

"Hey, it's not my business, not my case. All I want to do is catch who they want me to catch and find the bad guys. Special Operations is too weird for me," he replied.

Cornell shrugged. "Well, this place is way too boring for them to be here that long," he said and looked towards the hall. "Breakfast?" he asked. "Sure, I was just heading their myself," Rigin replied and the two of them made their way there doing their best to not attract any unwanted attention.

Jenny's phone dinged and it woke her up. "Damn it, I fell asleep," she said and cursed her lack of endurance. She looked at her phone and read the text. "Oh hell," she said and stood up and had no idea what to do now. She had to wait and see.

Sometimes panicking resulted in running right into the thing you were trying to avoid in the first place. Surely, they wouldn't announce a station wide search. If they were looking for something, that would be the first way to make sure it disappeared.

"I could just, yeah, that's what I'll do," she said and looked under the bed. The metal box was right where she left it. Dragging it back out from under the bed she picked it up. "Alright, we're going to sit here and wait," she said and sat on the bed. Now that the agents were in the outpost, the tension grew with every second. That door could have burst open at any second, she needed to be fast, not only fast but perfect.

Tense minutes of nothing but her staring at a door passed by and nothing changed. She looked at her phone. No new messages either. The walls of this room felt like they were closing in around her, it was so quiet now that every tiny, distant noise was putting her on edge.

She checked her phone and still, no texts. No updates. Then there was a sound. It felt as if it was coming from the outside. Maybe it was the sound of the blood rushing through her head. It was impossible to know. Maybe it was just better to give the heart up to Special Operations in the end? What was the worst that could happen?

No, she couldn't do that either. She'd get blamed for being Red Mirror, a vigilante and being thrown in any number of prisons. Cornell would be arrested too, maybe. There were so many bad situations that she was coming up with in her head, one right after another, that she almost missed the real footsteps coming down the hall.

They could have belonged to anyone, but this was no time to take any chances. Jenny concentrated. Despite the natural resistance of the iron, she disappeared in a golden plume of sparkling smoke, soon there was no trace of her at all. Jenny appeared on the roof behind a large and noisy air conditioning unit. She peeked around the corner to see a large red helicopter with two guards standing close by.

There were not many places to go from here. The iron was messing with her magic and teleporting was difficult. She was hoping that they wouldn't search up here much. She quietly slid the metal box under the air conditioning unit, it was almost too big to fit but she made it work all the same. Confident no one would look here for a little while, she teleported back into her room.

She heard a door shut down the hall. Then more footsteps before a knock on her door. Jenny got up and opened the door. "Yes?" she said to the agents. "Jenny Coldwell, we have full authority to search your room," the man said and stepped side, pushing her aside at the same time. "Well come on in," she replied sarcastically trying not to be pushed against the wall.

"I'm going to get right to the point, do you have anything you shouldn't?" he asked in a gruff tone. "No, I've only been here a day, maybe less, why?" she asked, and didn't have to act to sound annoyed. The man's expression didn't change. "Your partner wasn't in his room, there wasn't anything in there. We did detect some magical port energy from his room. It matches a Pixie's signature traits. What were you doing in there?" the man asked and Jenny shook her head.

"Oh, he had my sunglasses in his suitcase and I just had to zip over and get them. I had a tough day in the sun and I didn't feel like walking, sue me," she said and pointed to a pair of sunglasses laying on her pillow. The man just nodded. "Lazy, typical member of the force? Why walk when you can port twelve feet, right?" he asked, Jenny didn't like that, but it was just bait and she knew it.

"Are you done going through my things yet or is there something I can help you find?" she asked. He looked at her. "Seen anyone around with a metal box about so big?" he asked and measured it out with his hands, incorrectly. It was clear he'd never seen what he was looking for. "Nope, but then again I don't pay attention to what others do around here," she replied with a shrug.

"Well, if we find out you're lying about it, its at least ten years out in the Vault, you know that right. If you're sure you don't know anything, or if anything comes to mind, now's the time to speak up," he replied. She knew the rules and the punishments for breaking them. "Don't worry, I haven't seen anything like that. If I had I'd be sure to tell you. I got no reason to hide anything," she replied and tried to be as serious as she could manage.

"Sir, there's nothing in here," one of the searchers said tossed a blanket to the side beside the over turned mattress. "Thank you for your cooperation," the apparent leader replied, turned and walked back out not saying a word. As soon as the door closed, she let out a sigh of relief. If they had listening or magical recording devices in the rooms, they both would have been caught. Apparently, they were in the clear, at least for now.

Jenny pulled out her phone. 'We can't stay here tonight,' she texted to Cornell and pressed send.

Cornell's phone buzzed and he looked at it. "Tell me something I don't know," he said the message, mostly to himself. "Trouble at home?" Rigin asked and smirked. "Yeah, family issues. Is there a transport out tonight heading back to the city?" Cornell asked him right back. "Yeah, one is leaving this afternoon, about four I think," he replied and Cornell nodded.

"Thanks," he replied. 'Transport at four pm today,' he quickly texted back. He had a thing about spelling out numbers instead of just using them like most others tended to. 'k' Jenny texted him back, he cringed a little bit at the crude shorthand. 'No contact until its time to leave, no need to draw attention, keep it secret, keep it safe. See you at four,' Cornell typed out, and pressed send, then he deleted the conversation.

"These phones are going to give me nightmares," Cornell said as he put his away. "Yeah. Mocra comes out with a new one every couple of years it seems like. Its too expensive to keep up with them all," Rigin said as he finished his food. Cornell did a few seconds later.

"Well, I need to catch the bus, caught a new case. Bank robbery, pretty boring stuff but it pays the bills," Rigin said and Cornell nodded, "That it does," he replied and continued, "I'll see you later," he finished as Rigin got up and left.

Now Cornell needed to keep busy for a few hours. With all these agents creeping around, there was nothing he could do but just try to be normal and not attract any unwanted attention. He hated it, but it was for the best.

# Chapter Twelve

The hours droned by one at a time. With nothing productive to do time slowed to a crawl. He wondered how Jenny was doing as he sat in his room, watching the Kenders trial unfold, or try to. It was the slowest, dumbest thing he'd ever seen, but it was on the only two stations out here. Each station had a different bias on the matter. One thought he was guilty, the other was sure he was innocent. Neither station could come right out and say that, but it wasn't hard to tell.

Cornell didn't really care either way. He shut off the television and stared into the ceiling. Then his phone started to buzz again. He reached in his pocket and pulled it out. Thirty minutes left before it was time to go.

He got up and quickly gathered is minimal things and headed out the door. He walked down the hall and Jenny was there to meet him at the end of it. She looked just as tired as he did. "What's the plan?" she asked quietly. "I don't know," she answered herself with a slight yawn. Looking ahead she could see two guards searching everyone who was lining up to get to the transport.

"Can you make a distraction?" Cornell asked and she looked at him. "What did you have in mind?" she asked and he smiled. "Just a simple illusion, that's all. I'm going to head to the bathroom before we go, you make an illusion it so it looks like I walk out a few minutes later. I'll change clothes, get the item and magic back to the transport. No one will notice a thing if we pull it off," he said with a tired smile.

"You're insane, everything would have to go exactly right. It's too risky," she replied and the line to the transport began to move. "If you have a better suggestion I'd be interested in hearing it. Either my plan, or we risk spending another full night here with a pissed off vampire coming to get us," he said and shrugged all while trying to not attract any random listeners at the same time.

"Damn it, fine," she finally agreed to the plan and the two of them quickly moved towards the bathroom. "Just a few minutes. Good luck," Cornell said and walked in. "Hey, its on the roof, under the air conditioner, left side. Guards up there so be sneaky about it," she said quietly just before he disappeared behind the door. He nodded and slipped into the bathroom.

Walked to the stall on the farthest side, stepped inside. Then he pulled out his mirror. The red sparks covered his body and soon the red armor was around him again. Without wasting a second, he teleported to the roof. Everything was in black and white here in the mirror's realm. The guards were there, the helicopter was still there.

He moved to where she said it was going to be and sure enough, the box was still there, too. He pushed his hand through into normal reality and pulled the box out. It scraped against the metal. "Damn," he said and pulled the box through just a few seconds before the guards came around the corner.

"I swore I heard something," one said to the other. "I heard it too, but it could have just been this stupid thing. It's so damn old and noisy. I think it might be getting ready to blow up," the other replied. "Fine, I suppose you're right," the first one replied and the two of them moved back to their posts slowly. Cornell walked to the edge of the roof. Jenny and himself were walking in the line, just about to get on to the transport ship. "Come on, don't get caught now," he said and waited for the moment of failure.

Surprisingly, it didn't happen. He watched as her and the fake version of him walked on to the ship. He could see the magical aura from here and waited until they sat down. Thankfully Jenny thought far enough ahead to be one of the last ones on the ship so sitting together wasn't a problem.

It was soon enough they had sat down next to one another. "Okay, here goes nothing," he said and fell off the side of the outpost, disappearing half way down. Teleportation was often tricky, especially in situations like this. Cornell concentrated as hard as he could to hit the mark and found himself sitting inside of the illusion.

Quietly he dispelled the armor and slid the mirror back into his pocket. "I'm here, remove the spell," he whispered. Jenny relaxed and the illusion faded away. The box was in his lap and Jenny opened her mostly empty bag. Cornell slid it in without looking away and Jenny zipped it up. "You're awesome, that worked like a charm," he said and she groaned a little as the stress of one situation was beginning to fade only to be replaced by another.

"Don't worry once we get it to the city we'll be okay. Next, I need to find Zozo, apparently Loa says he knows the way to her old temple," Cornell said and Jenny shook her head. "How hard did that vampire hit you last night?" she asked wondering if the dream was the result of brain damage and not actually anything to do with a Goddess.

"Pretty hard, but I need to find him anyway. Goddess or not, the mission is the same. I know right where I am going to start looking once we get back," he replied. Then the transport ship came to life. Jenny looked out the window as they rose into the air. "I can't wait to get out of this desert," she said mostly to herself.

"Me either," he replied, and did his best not to think about what the Vampire was going to do to this place tonight looking for this box. If she could track it, she'd be led straight to this place, first, he figured it wouldn't be pretty. On the other hand, if she was in a hurry she might not waste any time and come straight for them. It was hard to tell but sundown wasn't far away. Everything would be known in just a few hours.

The ride to Echemos only took a few hours at a cruising speed at about three hundred miles an hour. Cornell kept expecting to be attacked somewhere along the way, but that never happened. Jenny was sleeping as they pulled into the station. "Hey," he said and poked her. "What?" she asked in a groan, not wanting to wake up.

"We're here, wake up," he replied and she sighed. "Fine, I guess," she replied. He wasn't sure how she could sleep but somehow, she did. The other passengers started to get up and leave. Cornell picked the bag. Jenny was still half asleep but forced herself to stand, then march down the aisle. Neither of them said anything to one another.

The second they got out if the transport and into the station they quickly separated themselves from the rest of the group. "Your place or mine," she asked and Cornell looked at the bag. "Neither. If that vampire is tracking this thing we need to go somewhere else, I have just the place," he said with a smile.

She rolled her eyes. "Oh man, I hate that place," she complained and wasn't happy about it. "It's the only choice we have right now. So, lets go," he replied, almost smiling at her annoyance but knew better than to do that if he didn't want to get punched.

The two of them walked around a corner, Cornell looked around and didn't see anyone. "Here we go," he said, put his hand on her shoulder. The two of them disappeared.

Everything was in black and white, all of the sounds were just a little off, too. They stood inside a darkly lit chamber that was full of things that had been collected over the years. "Why did you put your secret lair in another dimension, again?" she asked him. "First off, I didn't pick it. The mirror did and this is the same place that all the Red mirror bearers go. I've told you that a hundred times now," he said and she smiled.

"Yeah, I know, I'm just messing with you," she replied. The truth was, Cornell didn't know much about this place. Just that it was filled with all kinds of artifacts from the past. He suspected the mirror was an artifact prison of some kind originally, the stuff he didn't know could fill a book, he was sure. He wanted to just leave the heart here and forget about it, however an elder vampire could easily get into the Shadow Realm and find him. At least he thought so. This was only temporary, but for now it would do.

"So, what's the plan now?" she asked as he pulled the box out of the bag. "I am going to find Zozo, you are going to find out what the royal family knows about all of this and why they got Special Ops on the case. For all we know they were trying to get the thing too," he replied as he set the metal box on the table.

"Wait, you expect me to go up to the castle and just start, what, asking questions?" she asked and wasn't quite sure what he meant by finding out. "This one is going to be off the books, you're a Pixie. You can shrink down to super tiny sizes and learn things. Think of it as an adventure we can tell our kids someday," he replied and she shook her head.

"If I get caught it's going to be worse than prison time," she replied and he knew that. "Well, its up to you. I know you can do it. I believe in you. I'm sure you can even get one of them to talk with a one of those nifty illusion spells of yours," he replied trying to think of reasons for her to go.

"Do you really trust some vision you had, you do know that the vision or dream could had just been created by some nasty desert town water, too. I mean finding Zozo and going to Loa's old temple. Doesn't that seem just a little bit crazy to you?" she asked and he shrugged.

"No, it seems like it's entirely crazy, but what else am I going to do. We can't leave it here for too long. We can destroy the heart of one of the worst people in the world, ending the threat forever. I say it is worth a shot, don't you?" he asked right back and she rolled her eyes. "Fine, I guess. I'll go home, get some sleep then at first light, get to work," she said and he smiled. "Don't forget to check in at work, keep up normal appearances," he said and she shook her head.

"I'm not an idiot," she replied and continued, "don't forget to do the same, and if you wouldn't mind. I'd like a portal out of here," she said. He nodded and waved his left hand. A long slit was cut open in the black and white world, it opened up. "I'll even take you home," he said. Just as he said it she looked into her own apartment.

"Are you sure you don't want to come over, it's barely past midnight," she said with a smile. "Not tonight, need to sleep to make sure we have enough energy to do what we need to do," he said, disappointed. "Oh, fine," she replied and stepped through the portal and waved as it closed behind her. He nodded with a smile, then she was gone.

"Damn it, we are so screwed," he said to himself seconds later.

# Chapter Thirteen

Cornell stepped into his own apartment, he left the box behind in the Shadow realm. He walked forward and made it to his chair that was in front of his television and turned it on as he sat down and set his bag down beside him.

"Today, Pen Kenders, proclaimed his innocence yet again and- "he turned the channel. "I am so sick of that crap," he said to himself.

"We are joining a situation in progress, I still can't believe what I'm seeing here, Jim," a man said, but no one was visible. Instead the camera was up in the air, pointed down on what appeared to be a war zone of some kind. In the dark, and with the building on fire. It was hard to even know what anyone was looking at. Then it hit him. "Outpost," he said in shock.

"Yeah Ron, we're out here over Outpost thirteen of the Mystic Force has been devastated by something. We don't know what could have caused this but as of right now I can't see how any-one might have lived through this. Anyone watching this right now, please, pray for a miracle, because right now we need one," Ron said and Cornell shut off the television.

He had expected something, but not that. Now he wished that he would have at least gotten the vampire's name before bailing like he did. He was so tired right now, but time was running out. That monster was likely on a direct path straight to the city. There was no telling what kind of damage she would do, or if she could even be stopped.

Cornell opened his bag and pulled out the severed hand. "Might as well talk to you some more. Maybe you missed a few details," he said to the hand and set it on the table in front of him. "Zintero Mosk Loen," he said and raised his left hand. The red glow returned and soon enough the elf woman appeared.

"It feels even better if you just move it up a little and—wait," she said and looked around. "Oh, hell it's you again, could you please lose my hand. Being summoned like this is annoying. After you're dead you don't need to answer questions anymore. Its one of the perks of being dead," she said to him and glared. She was still wearing the same thing as the last time.

"Nice to see you too," he replied. "What's your name?" he asked right away. "I'm Kaylen Sarno, you know, if we would have met when we were alive you totally would have had a chance," she said and shook his head. "Thanks Kaylen. I suppose I should tell you why you and your friends were killed," he replied.

"Oh, you figured it out, was it something interesting at least?" she asked him and crossed her arms. "You could say that. Someone killed you for your blood. They used it for a lock," he said, he knew she was confused. "Old school blood lock. It was used to seal up the heart of the old vampire lord. You know, the one who was in charge of the war," he said as if it meant something. Kaylen just shrugged. "I failed history class, but that sounds pretty bad," she said.

"Yeah, its bad. Sort of end of the world bad, but that seems to be the new trending thing these days," Cornell replied. "Nah, the world won't end. I think you'll stop it long before it gets that bad," she said with a smile and he shrugged.

"I don't want to keep you much longer. Do you remember where the Poison Cup was at? I mean, all you have to do is get close. It's not like you need an exact location. Anywhere close will do," he said. "Yeah, Echemos, Black Dust or Sand section I think they call it. You know the place?" she asked and he rolled his eyes. "Of course it was there. It literally couldn't have been anywhere else," he replied and blamed his tired mind in not even thinking about it.

"Well its in the old part, we thought it was kind of strange, but in Black Dust, everything is a little off so we were okay with it. I swear after that I don't know anything," she said and frowned. "You've been a great help, Kaylen. I'm going to destroy the hand so you can have peace, no one will be able to summon you again," he replied and she looked away.

"Wait, my parents. Could you keep me around long enough, until after the, whatever this is, is over? So I can say good bye," she asked and Cornell wasn't sure this was a good idea. "Well, since you asked so nice I'll think about it. Until then. Enjoy Sarjenia," he said. "I'll see you soon," she replied with an almost creepy smile and with a wave of his hand, she faded away back to the other side.

Cornell thought about it. The vampire wouldn't get here at least until tomorrow night. The distance was too great with out a transport. If he was going to investigate the Black Sand sector of town, he was going to need to have a clear mind. Cornell decided to go to be and worry about whatever came next when it got here. These problems weren't going to go away on their own. He also thought he should feel paranoid.

A crazy elder vampire on his trail didn't have anything good in store for him or his immediate future. She could show up at his place at any time. It didn't matter to him, not right now. He took his old clothes off in a hurry as he made his way to the shower. A few minutes later he was in bed, passed out under a thin blanket.

"So, necromancer. You think you can just stroll in to things you don't understand and mess everything up?" a voice said to him. Cornell knew he was dreaming, but none of this felt very restful. "Who is it this time?" he asked and looked around, but didn't see anyone, or anything but a green sky and black sand as far as he could see.

"No, seriously. I am sick of people invading my dreams so out with it already," he said. "We've already met, back in the chamber. I am coming for you. Right now. As you sleep somewhere in that city, unprotected. I am making my way too you," the voice said. Cornell rolled his eyes. "Theatrics are pointless, vampire. You'd think one as old as yourself would understand that by now?" he asked wondering how she found out at all. That was a scarier than any nightmare.

Then she stood in front of him. Eyes burning bright blue, dressed in a black shroud of mist that blew in a wind he couldn't feel. "I understand that I was moments away from achieving greatness and you stole it," she said, but the words felt more like a voice coming from the inside of his head. "Greatness, you want to bring a monster back into the world, that's your idea of greatness?" he asked again.

"What I do, I do for the entire vampire race. We won't be slaves to mortals any longer," she screamed and the voice was enough to wake him up. It was still dark, but the first rays of the sun were barely beginning to light up the night sky. "Figures she'd go away with the dawn," he mumbled to himself, turned over and went back to sleep.

# Chapter Fourteen

Jenny woke up with a start after a fitful sleep. She expected to see a razor fanged vampire holding her in their hand. But she was in her room, right where she fell asleep. Jenny stretched, loosening up before she stood up on the edge of the desk. With a jump she fell off the edge of the desk and grew to her normal size instantly. The morning routine only took about a half hour, then he was out of the shower and feeling pretty good when she remembered her so called mission.

"Damn," she said as she walked to the computer and sat down in the chair and turned the thing on. It was a quick thing to log into her work site to check her messages. There were no new messages. "Weird," she said to herself and thought that maybe this had something to do with being pulled off that case.

The rays of the sun streaming through her window had just started, the morning was here. Yet even now, for some reason, she felt as if she was running out of time. Once the sun was gone, there was no telling what kind of nightmares were in store. It was time to get ready to go to the castle and see what there was to find out. She turned the screen off, stood up walked to the door. For a brief second, she imagined herself opening this door and an explosion going off, or someone waiting behind it to kill her.

She opened the door and none of those things happened. The only thing waiting for her was the same old basic brown hallway that had always been there, at least this time. Before anything else, she had to get some breakfast on the way, she was starving.

Jenny lived in the Sunbeam sector of Echemos, and in all of Sunbeam, there was only one place that she liked to eat more than any other. That place was called Sherrie's Diner and in that brief thought, that was where she decided to go today. She didn't feel like teleporting so she stepped into the hall, closed and locked the door behind her. It was a quick trip down the hall and outside. Then she took to the sky. Flying up and over the city.

Echemos was just coming back to life under the hot rays of the sun. Noises from the city, cars, trucks and other things. She saw others like her flying through the air, going to their various places. People teleporting from place to place. This city was perfect for a woman like Jenny. It didn't matter what you were, the desert was a great place to live for magic users of all races. She ignored them and made her way to the diner. She smiled when she saw it, and right now the place wasn't that busy either. All good news so far, today.

She landed in the parking lot and walked to the door, opened it and stepped inside. Immediately the smells and sounds of the place made her feel relaxed. "Hey there, Jen, welcome back," Sherrie said and she nodded. "I thought I was going to be longer than I was but as it turned out, we got swiped," Jenny replied.

"Swiped?" Sherrie asked as they moved to the bar. "Yeah, canned, replaced. We were working the case, then orders came down from up on high," she said and pointed towards the castle. It was made of sunstone and when the actual sun hit it, the thing appeared as if it was made out of pure gold for most of the day.

"You're kidding me. The royals shut you down?" she asked and shook her head as Jenny sat down. "Yep, that's how it all went down. No reasons, it just was done. Their special police people took over the case, and that's all I know," she replied and Sherrie shook her head.

"So, the usual to cheer you up then?" she asked and Jenny nodded. "Yeah, that'll be just fine," Jenny replied. It was then she saw the television behind the bar and the scenes it was showing. "Oh, Loa, what is this all about?" she asked and Sherrie looked at the television, it was muted so she turned the volume up.

"Outpost Thirteen is destroyed, as we've been reporting on since late last night, we don't know how many people were lost in the fire yet but this tragic accident is," Jenny shut the tv off with a snap of her fingers and buried her face with her hands for a few seconds. "I was there just hours before that happened," she said and continued, "that could have been me," she finished. Her halfway good day was just wrecked by the news.

"Oh, dear, but you got lucky at least. Tell you what, today's breakfast is on the house," she said and Jenny tried to smile. "Thanks," she replied. All she could think about is how many detectives were torched last night and now it made sense as to why she didn't get any messages. It was odd that there wasn't a network wide bulletin about it the ordeal either. Sherrie walked away as someone else came in. Jenny turned to look at the castle and narrowed her eyes a little, due to the glare.

A few minutes past and a waitress came back to Jenny with a plate. "One Dragon Omelet with a side of fried potatoes, and a nice Zolro Juice to drink," she said. Overly happy almost for the situation Jenny was dealing with. Everyone had different lives. Tragedy in one person's world was just another news story to another and right now they were both helpless to do anything about it.

"Thank you," Jenny replied and the waitress walked away. Jenny proceed to eat her meal, it tasted just as great as all the other times she had it. Spicy, just how she liked it. It didn't take very long to eat the whole thing and before she knew it, it was all gone. The food made her feel a little better now.

Now she had work to do. "Sherrie, thanks again for the meal. I'll see you later," Jenny said and Sherrie stuck her head out the double doors leading to the back. "Alright, you take care and come back again soon," she replied and disappeared in the back just as fast.

Jenny got up and walked out of the Diner. Now, the hard part of the day began. "Damn it Cornell, how come you always get the easy stuff," she complained to herself, but wasn't sure that tracking down a known, thought to be dead, bad guy was any better of an option. Actually, the more she thought about it, the less she wanted to be in his shoes right now.

Taking to the air and getting to the castle was easy. However, getting inside was the harder part. It was warded from magical entry of all kinds. She was sure there were other kinds of security too, but one thing at a time.

She flew in the direction the castle and knew that to get inside, someone would have to let her inside. The big and obvious front door wasn't going to work. Even at small size, the cameras would pick her up. She watched a documentary on the castle once. It was pretty interesting and that gave her an idea. She flew up and over the castle as she shrank down to her normal pixie size of just a couple of inches.

There was a stationary camera there on the corner of the roof, she pointed at it and blasted it with twin beams of dark orange flame. The camera wires were hit and sparks flew for a couple of seconds before the thing powered down. Now, all she could do is watch and wait. The wait was not a long one.

She saw a hatch open up from the roof and a man in a grey uniform came out. "Damn this camera, this is the third time this week," he muttered to himself as he pulled his tools out behind him, set it on the roof. Then he propped the hatch open just after he walked towards the broken machine. "Oh, come on, melted this time. Why is it melted?" he asked and looked around for a good reason for it but didn't see anything. Jenny wondered if he looked up, if he would see her.

Thankfully he didn't look up and got to work. Jenny took her chance and flew straight into the open hatch. After this, she had no idea where to go next. The tunnels at this size might has well have been infinite abysses with lights over head every so often. But the long, dark times in between didn't pass quickly.

Jenny flew around for so many minutes, but being lost in the tunnels made it feel like hours. Suddenly a door opened up and she shot around a corner. It was another worker in a gray uniform. Jenny flew low to the ground and made it through the door before it closed. It was only a few seconds through that room to the other side. That door was almost closed before she slipped through the cracks and found herself in one of the many hallways of the castle, alone.

"From one maze into another," she said and looked both ways. Neither of them seemed like they would be going anywhere useful and there weren't any signs to tell people where to go. That made sense, she supposed. No one unauthorized was supposed to be here anyway so she listened for voices. Where there were people, there was information, at least she hoped so.

Jenny went left and didn't know where this was going to lead. She flew high, her wings nearly touching the ceiling as she flew. People were talking and to her it felt as if it was an angry conversation. It only took a few minutes flying until she came to the edge of a door. The voices were coming from here. It was someone's office. The name on the door read 'Sir Hiram Gyl, Director of Special Operations.' Jenny couldn't believe her actual luck, maybe Loa was helping them after all.

"I am going to tell you again, we didn't have anything to do with your outpost being blown up," a voice said, raised. It must have been Hiram. "The hell you didn't, one day after you took the case it all went bad. Explain that to me again," Joe said. Jenny knew that voice. It was Blackthorn, chief of the Mystic Force.

"An unknown agent is after the heart. We think it's the Cansema Cult, but we don't know anything yet. Just let us do our job," Hiram said. "Your job? No one knows what your job is, what am I supposed to tell the families of the ones we lost. Sorry, your people were killed by someone we don't know and can't find. But don't worry. We're depending on the secret police no one knows anything about to do their best," Joe replied and there was silence.

"Tell them what ever will help them sleep at night, I don't care because they aren't my problem," Hiram said, his voice returning to its calm demeanor. There was more nothing from behind the door. "Fine," Joe said in a voice that was restrained. The chair slid back then a few seconds later the door Jenny was by opened up.

Apart of her just wanted to go inside the office and blast that guy in the face, but there might not be anyway out and the risk was too high of failure. Joe stormed out of the office and walked down the hall. The door closed behind him. Jenny didn't know what a Cansema cult was exactly, but the name sounded familiar to her. She knew that this was a new clue, so she had to figure out what it meant, but first she had to find a way out of here.

# Chapter Fifteen

Cornell woke up from a fitful rest, the sun was shining through the window. There was no vampire standing over him so he supposed it wasn't all bad. He got up and spent the next thirty minutes taking care of all the morning stuff he did every day. He just about called Jenny but decided against it. She didn't need anymore pressure from him or anyone else.

He walked to the computer and turned it on. It only took a few seconds to get to the worksite, but once he did he saw there were no messages. He was pretty sure it had something to do with the attack last night. It was pretty unusual, not even a standing order was issued. This made it easier to do what he needed to get done today.

He grabbed the red mirror and stuck it in his pocket. He had to go to the one place where you didn't want to bring your car unless you wanted it stripped, he'd get there with magic instead. He didn't like teleportation so much but sometimes you just didn't have a choice. Not wasting anymore time he made sure he door was locked one more time, then disappeared as he summoned a blue aura with a wave of his hand.

Cornell reappeared in an alleyway where the sun hadn't yet reached. He looked around and was happy his life detection spell worked this time.

He walked out of the alleyway and had no idea where to go next. Cornell walked right, not knowing where to go and hoped for the best. His best bet was to find a local and see if they knew anything. He walked for ten minutes down the road not seeing anyone. He felt a little frustrated at his situation. Cornell hated this part of town it was nothing more than a cesspool. He stopped and looked across the street. 'King Richard's Head' was open, the old sign hung in the window.

"Better than nothing," he said and walked across the empty street to the place. He walked inside and was surprised to see that the place wasn't empty. Elves, some Humans and even an Orc in the corner, that one was far from home.

Cornell walked right to the counter and a man was there to meet him. It wasn't anyone named Richard, according to the name tag, it was Ted. "Welcome to the head, how can I help you. Table or Booth?" the man asked and Cornell smiled. "Information," he said and pulled out his Mystic Force badge. Ted nodded as he saw it. "I don't what I can help with, Detective. I spend all my time keeping this place from falling apart," he replied.

"Don't sell yourself short just yet. I'm looking for a place called The Poison Cup, or something like that. Know of any place by that name, Ted," Cornell said with a smile. He was watching every move Ted was making now. He knew Black Sand people didn't rat on their own people very often. Ted was nervous, his eyes widened a little. "There are so many clubs that come and go around here, its hard to keep track of them all," Ted replied.

"Really, that fast?" Cornell asked. He knew that much was true but even if it was, someone must have seen something. "Yeah, that fast. Some are one-night specials. Pop up clubs, you know. Magical places. Totally illegal but they happen. No one cares what happens here," Ted said, still nervous, but he was sure now that it wasn't him that was making him nervous.

"Oh, well if you think of something else be sure to let me know. Here's my card," he said and a white business card appeared in his left hand. Cornell put it on the counter and slid it in his direction. "Yeah, sure," Ted replied and grabbed the card, sliding it his pocket quickly. Cornell nodded, turned around and left the place. Not wasting anytime, he slipped around the corner and waited. He had a lot of tricks that went against the official code of the Mystic Force. Listening devices with out a warrant was one of them.

On the other hand, this wasn't an official investigation anymore. He pulled his business card out of his pocket and leaned against the wall.

"What'd the cop want?" a voice asked, "He wanted to know about The Poison Cup," Ted replied. "Did you tell him anything," the other voice asked. "No, I don't know anything. I just said that these clubs can disappear overnight, that's all," Ted replied. "And you didn't tell him anything else you're sure. If you lied to me, you know what happens," the other voice replied.

"Damn it man, I didn't talk about Tsuba. I didn't say anything. You would have known anyway, remember the ward your meathead friend put on my neck. It would have killed me if I talked to anyone but you. You know that. Give me a break already I won't risk it," Ted almost whispered. "Oh yeah, I forgot, you keep working, and Mr. Moreno will knock off a couple of weeks off your debt, if you can manage to stop racking so much up," the man said.

Cornell hated the Moreno family. He's dealt with them for years as a detective and the Red Mirror. He's yet to take them down after all this time despite all of his power. He didn't know what Tsuba was supposed to be, but right now there was some Moreno muscle in this place and he was about to be in the mood for a quick chat.

He looked around and saw no one. He pulled out the mirror and quickly transformed into his armored form, then stepped into the shadow realm. The wall in front of him was less solid than it appeared here, he stepped through that as if he were a ghost. Not much had changed in here and there was no sign of the muscle.

He was likely in the back somewhere. He felt eyes on him and looked to the corner. The Orc was staring right at him. They could see into the shadow realm, well not all of them but its been know to happen. On the other hand, there was a good chance that this guy was high on Ice Brain too and was seeing things. After a few seconds of the constant, stone cold gaze was being unbroken Cornell decided it was the drugs and continued his search.

The strolled through the counter and the walls to head to the back. Everyone in the back was a mess. Their uniforms, if you could call it that had been stained with various colors. Everyone here looked like they were exhausted, then he saw why. Every-one one of them had black shackle around their left ankles. This was a Moreno slavery front. They called it a debt repayment center.

There he was, a big troll halfling in a suit. He wasn't sure what he was mixed with but this guy was a brute. Cornell didn't know who this guy was, but he didn't care either. He walked through the kitchen, invisible like a ghost. Cornell thought that sometimes this was a lot unfair, on the other hand they were complete monsters that the law couldn't seem to touch.

Cornell was a big guy but this troll mixed thing was taller that him, even like this. Cornell stepped behind the big guy and out of the shadow realm. "Hey there, have a minute?" he asked in his altered voice. The man jumped forward as he spun around. "You're real, really?" he asked and his eyes widened. "Yep, afraid so," Cornell replied.

For a second the man stared at the red urban legend in front of him then tried to react by running away. Cornell lunged for-ward, grabbed the enforcer and the two of them disappeared.

"Where am I?" the man asked as he stumbled. "Shadow realm," Cornell replied and crossed his arms. All around them were people still confused about what was going on, unsure what to do next.

"Red Mirror is it, come on. I don't want to be here. What do you want?" the man asked in a much softer voice than before. "First. Tsuba, what is it?" Cornell asked him and crossed his arms. "I don't know anything about that," the man asked and Cornell was in no mood for games, and he didn't have the time for it. He outstretched his hand and blasted the man in the chest sending him through the building. As he flew, he wrecked nothing but made it all the way to the outside. Cornell was already there when he was trying to get up.

"I have no time for games, if you don't tell me what I want to know right now, I'm leaving you here," he said and the panic in the man's eyes grew. "No, you can't leave me here," he cried out and continued. "Tsuba is a building the family owns. I don't know why they call it that but that's what it is. I think it's where they keep the money before its transferred. I don't know where it is. Please send me back," the man said, nearly in tears. He'd only heard stories of the Shadow Realm and the Red Mirror. Now he was faced with dealing with both of them.

Cornell was always surprised when these tough guys broke down like this. Most of them were all big and bad when they were confronted with people who couldn't fight back. Once they were out matched they all broke down. Of course, most of the stories people told about him were actually true.

"Send you back. You enslaved all those people and worked for people who make money on the blood of innocent people. You think you deserve mercy. Of course you do. Why not. One more thing. Tell me about the Poison cup. A club around here somewhere?" Cornell asked. The man backed away. "I can't, she'll kill me," he said in a growing panic.

"You think I won't, really. You people, you always say that line but some how you think that I can't do things to you that make death feel like a paradise in comparison. Now talk before you really piss me off," Cornell said and took a step closer.

"All I know is that it was a pop-up club. Velima made a deal with Mr. Moreno to make it happen. I worked security that night. I don't know anything else," he said and Cornell smiled under that helmet. "The club might not be there anymore, but I am sure the building it was hosted in is. Start walking," Cornell said and the man shook his head. "Yeah, sure. I know the way," he said and the two of them moved forward.

Walking through the shadow realm was a creepy experience. The oversized enforcer of the mob cringed at each step that echoed endlessly into the distance. "If you walk any slower you're going to attract the things that live here, move faster," Cornell said, frustrated already, feeling like he was wasting time.

"It's not far, just around the corner here," the man said just as he started to turn the corner. "Yeah, good," Cornell replied and sure enough the two of them came to a building. It was tall, made out of gray stone. There was no telling how long it had been here. It was also almost completely covered with formless, writhing shadow things.

"They really like this place," Cornell said but the man backed off. "One more thing. The slaves back at the entrance, how do we release them?" he asked. "Once I'm back I'll do it, the wards are connected to my lifeforce. I'll break the spell once you let me go," he said and Cornell shook his head. "I know I can trust you, but you know what?" Cornell asked and briefly considered to kick him into the mass of shadows.

"If I come back and a single slave is there. I'm going to find you and feed you this mass one piece at a time, do you understand?" he asked and the man kept backing off, terrified at the site of the shadowy things.

"I understand," he managed to whisper. Cornell grabbed him by the shoulder and threw him forward. The man screamed as he fell forward into the mass, then through the dimensional barrier into his home world. The man slowly opened his eyes and found that color had returned to the world and he was, at least for now, safe.

Cornell watched the man get up and run away as fast as he could around the corner. He wasn't kidding. If he came back and the slaves were still there, he was going to feed him to the shadow things. Cornell stepped out of the shadow realm and moved forward into the stone building.

The door was old, it didn't belong to a club. This felt more like the ancient fortresses of old. It didn't surprise him too much. Echemos was a city of layers. No one really knew how far down it went, just that each civilization was built on top of the older ones, and the sands just kept rising around it. Someday all of this would be forgotten as well. He pushed the heavy brown door opened with surprising ease.

It was black inside. If this was a club of any kind it was impossible to tell now. Dust covered everything, this was a long dead place and it was no wonder the shadow realm creatures liked it here. They liked old and dead things the most. Finding clues here was going to be difficult at best. "Nortex" Cornell said and a red pulse flew forward from his body. Cornell expected to find footprints, traces of life. Something he could recognize.

What he found was much more interesting. There at the back of the room a door's outline began to shine red. It wasn't visible by normal means. Cornell always thought using magic to find things was cheating when he first started this job, however, he soon decided that the bad guys used it all the time and followed no rules at all so he stopped feeling that way after a few weeks on the job.

He walked towards the door and looked for a way to open the thing, but there didn't seem to be anyway to do it. He didn't even know what way the door opened. He put his left hand against it and at once an invisible ward fired off a charge of energy. It was enough to even make him feel the pain through the magical armor.

He pulled his hand back and the pain faded immediately. "Damn wards," he said. Due to the magical nature of his armor, despite how powerful it was, it still had to obey the basic rules of magic. "Time for plan B, I guess," he said to himself and dispelled his armor. The door was still there, the outline still glowed faintly. He put his hands against the door. One on each side then he started to push. At first, nothing happened. It was as solid as a real wall, but still, he knew it had to move.

"Come on you stupid thing open up," he said and pushed harder, but still it didn't budge an inch. "Now what am I supposed to do?" he asked himself as he gave up to think of a new plan. Then it occurred to him that maybe the door had a password. But that could have literally been anything. "Zozo," he said, but nothing happened. Cornell thought about it a little more, all the names and connections he had heard up to this point.

Evil was lots of things. Arrogant was usually top of the list. The enforcer mentioned a name, but he couldn't remember what it was, not exactly. "Velma," he said, nothing. It started with a V, what was it? "Valentine, no, too many letters," he said and continued to think, trying to remember what that name was. "Vlad?" he asked, but that wasn't right, it was too short. Then it came to him. "Velima," he said and the door cracked, then silently swung out opened out towards him.

It revealed a long winding staircase into the black depths. "Oh, I just love staircases into hell," he whispered. With the ward broken and he was free to proceed, he transformed back into his armored form and began to walk down the stairs as quietly as he could. On one side was a stone wall, on the other a plunge into darkness. He would have jumped straight into the dark, but having no idea what was waiting down there, it was best to take his time.

The stairs all had sand on them that slightly crunched underfoot. He thought that was a little strange but did his best to ignore it. In the dark time seemed to lose all meaning and distance was impossible to judge, even with his enhanced vision there was something unnatural about this darkness.

Then after what felt like hours there was a dim light at the bottom of the stairs. Light meant life, the dead didn't need the light. So not wasting anymore time he floated off the stairs and quietly made his way down to the light. The entryway was an ancient arch with writing on it he couldn't read, but it wasn't warded as far as he could tell.

Cornell walked into the room and immediately, it was hot, he could feel the fire on the other side of the room through his armor. "Damn it," he whispered to himself. Only a few things could make fire this hot.

A figure was sitting in a chair, facing the fire. A green cloak was hanging on the wall. Cornell looked around the room for details, traps, anything that might have been useful or a threat. He didn't see much of anything in here.

"You found me," the figure said, but he didn't get up. It was Zozo's voice. "You were hard to miss. Care to explain, I don't know, everything?" Cornell asked and the figure turned around. His eyes still blazed with that green fire. "Sure, I guess I can do that for an old friend," he said and Cornell cringed, he didn't know why he said that. He wasn't going to let him know it got to him.

"Start talking, time is limited," Cornell replied. "Yes, mirror, it is limited. It is so limited, you have no idea. I guess it all started last year," Zozo replied and started in on a long story. "Stop, stick to the details, names, reasons. Important stuff. I didn't come here to hear a long winded tale," Cornell said and Zozo shook his head.

"What kind of detective doesn't want to hear the whole story?" he asked with a smile. "One who's in a hurry now get on with it," Cornell replied crossing his arms. "Velima came to me to send a message to you, she needed me to dump six bodies in some dirt town to get your attention. Paid me in gold to do it. I told her you were a Necromancer, she needed one. A delightful elder vampire by all accounts," Zozo said.

"You told her, just how much did you end up telling her?" Cornell asked, worried a little bit now. "Nothing that would spoil the fun. Just that, she just needed one to open that silly door," Zozo said with a smile, his eyes burned a little more brightly.

"Do you know what was behind that door?" Cornell asked and Zozo shrugged. "Who knows. I didn't ask or care, money was good enough reason for me to help," he replied with that same smile. "Damn it, it was the heart of the old vampire King. The one who waged the war. The vampire wants to bring back the old days," Cornell said and Zozo shook his head.

"I was pretty sure that," Cornell cut him off. "It was a lie, all of it apparently. I don't know what went down exactly back then but it doesn't matter now," Cornell said and Zozo looked away. "Maybe a war wouldn't be so bad, one hundred years of peace has turned the kingdoms into weak shells of themselves. Maybe we need some hard times after all," he said and Cornell shook his head. "You're insane. Anyway, enough small talk. I'm only here because I need your help," Cornell said and Zozo was confused.

"My help, how could I help you. No, better question, why would I help you at all?" he asked and Cornell shrugged. "I had a dream, a vision I think. Loa said you knew the way to her old temple and I could destroy the vampire heart there," he replied and Zozo nodded. "You've been hitting the Chillweed a little too hard, but as it so happens, yes. I know the way to the temple," he replied and leaned back into his chair.

"Can you get me there?" he asked and Zozo smiled. "I can, but I won't. After you screwed me over with your self appointed hero routine I was forced to hide here, in the ruins of this old mage tower. The world thinks I'm dead and I might as well stay that way," he replied with a smile. Cornell thought about it.

"It's Loa's first temple. There must be something in that place that you want. If you help me get there I'll, well, I'll help you get it," Cornell said and knew he'd regret that in the future. "There is something there that I want, but can't get. You're not going to stab me in the back if we go. You, on your honor as a hero, won't betray me in anyway?" Zozo asked and Cornell looked into the fire that was burning beside the one in the chair.

"Yes," he replied. "I promise," he finished. Zozo smiled. "Well then, by all means let's get started," he said as he stood up. The flames in the fireplace exploded outwards and wrapped around Zozo's body, being absorbed in his body. He outstretched his hands and the green cloak flew out and wrapped around him.

"Why the green cloak?" Cornell asked. "I don't know. I just picked it up somewhere and liked it, I think I was just jealous of your cape," he replied. Cornell shook his head. "The cape look was terrible, I figured out how to turn that thing off," Cornell replied. Zozo frowned in disappointment. "So, when do we leave?" he asked and Cornell looked towards the stairs. "Now," he replied, floated off the ground and took off back through the entrance. "Always so dramatic," Zozo said and followed him.

# Chapter Sixteen

Jenny made it out of the castle and was flying through the air, still at her normal size of just a few inches tall when her phone rang. She picked it up and answered it. "Hey," she said. "You actually found him, so much for being dead," she replied. "Alright, I'll meet you there in a few minutes," she replied and hung up the phone. There was no point in talking too much on the phone, there was no telling who might be listening in these days.

Cornell and Zozo were on the top of the Tsuba building, waiting. "So, you're still seeing the Pixie?" Zozo asked. "Yeah. If you try to hurt her I'll kill you, again," he replied. "Oh, you're still sore about all that. It's all boring now. I'd need to find new ways to try and break you," Zozo said and Cornell didn't like where this conversation was heading.

"Tell me about the temple," Cornell said and Zozo looked into the sky, towards the west. "It's outside the wall. Pretty far too. Only idiots, desperate people and, well, me, go that far. The temple is old, sinking into the sand. Last time I was there, however, the cosmic flame of Loa burned in the center of the place. Bright purple and green, so many colors at once," he replied.

"Why did you go there in the first place?" Cornell asked and Zozo smiled. "I went for the Book. It has lots of titles, but I always called it my dream. The most powerful fire spells in the world. Written by a fire elemental, and Loa herself. With it, I could have literally done anything I wanted," he said with a sigh. Then it occurred to Cornell that the promise that he made was going to set the whole world on fire. Now he was regretting all of this.

"Oh, good. An ultimate power tome of destruction in the hands of a crazy person, just what we all need," Cornell replied and Zozo laughed. "Insane, me. I doubt it. No crazier than you playing hero with an ancient artifact you found on a case," Zozo replied. Cornell was about to reply when Jenny flew down in a mote of light behind Cornell and expanded to her human sized form.

"Professor," Jenny said and nodded. "I haven't been called that in a long time. So good of you to remember," Zozo replied and she narrowed her eyes. "Okay, so how are we getting to where we need to go?" Jenny asked them, realizing now that they had no plan at all.

"Two Mystic Force detectives and one misunderstood professor, we make a great group. Maybe we should try not attracting too much attention?" Zozo asked and Cornell agreed with him on that point. "We could just fly over the walls," Jenny suggested. "We could, but your buddies would see us," Zozo said and Cornell shook his head. "We can travel through the shadow realm, but if we are going do it, I'd rather not do it from this building, it's, well, its busy," Cornell added nervously, he knew Jenny hated the things in the shadow realm.

"I don't like that place either," Zozo replied. He knew it was too easy to be left there, with all of the nasty shadow beasts. "Well, it's not safe here and once the sun goes down that vampire will be on us in no time, we should leave now," Cornell said, he was coming up with an idea on how to do it, too.

"Fine, I guess you're right," Zozo said and continued. "We need to get over the Scorched wall, then we have a long trek through the desert. Are you sure you just want to try and fly there. If I were you, I'm not, but if I was. I'd suggest trying to get some kind of transport to conserve energy, just a thought," Zozo said with a shrug.

"Fine, I get your point, what kind of transport are we going to need?" Jenny asked. "Class two, at least. Something that can take a hit. Monsters live on the Outside and we will need some protection. Supplies too, water, food, healing stuff. We should cover all the basis. I know we all have these nifty powers, but it might be good to not only rely on them. You never know what you're going to meet out there," Zozo said. "Fine. I think I know where to get a nice ride that'll work," Cornell said and now he couldn't wait to get it started.

"I can go shopping for stuff, what are you going to do, fire-bug?" Jenny asked him. "I'm going to stay here, out of sight. If anyone out there sees and recognizes me and this gets a lot more complicated than it needs to be. Don't worry. I don't have anywhere else to go, I'll be here when you get back," he said with a smile. Jenny had questions for him about what happened in Larenville but now wasn't the time.

"You better be, I don't have time to hunt you down again," Cornell replied, with that him and Jenny flew off in opposite directions. "Don't waste too much time," Zozo said, turned and looked out over the city. From here he could see a lot of it, and he imagined it all covered in the cleansing fire. He smiled knowing it that wouldn't be long now if everything went according to plan.

Jenny didn't have a list of the things she needed. Common sense said that food and water was on the top of that list she didn't have and knew how to get the supplies she needed the quickest. Jenny flew to the Mystic Force department headquarters. It was in the Desert Wind district of the city. It didn't take more than fifteen minutes to get there at top speed.

The headquarters was the tallest building in the sector. It shot into the air like a grey spike covered in black windows. However, there was almost no indication that this was the actual main office on the outside of the building. Jenny landed on the roof of the building. The guard on the roof was startled for a second. "Woah, it's just me," she said and the man smiled. "Oh, hey Coldwell. You're lucky I know you so well because it doesn't look like you have your ID with you," he said and she panicked inside a little. In all the stress, she forgot that at home.

"Well, lucky me," she replied. "Do you want to see it because I can go home and get it," Jenny said and the guard smiled, his pale blue eyes glinted in the bright sun. "Nope, go on in. If it was an illusion spell or anything the wards would have caught it," he said and opened the door. "Thanks, Bill," she said and walked through the open door. He closed it behind her and wondered if she'd ever realize his name was Bob and not Bill.

Jenny walked straight to the elevator and got inside and pushed the third floor button. The ride there wasn't very long and she got out. There were many desks and people on this floor. Everyone appeared to be calm despite the destruction of the outpost. She made her way to the supply desk. A woman was sitting there, an Ogre who was also, very clearly a vampire. "Just wonderful," Jenny whispered to herself as she approached and had lots of questions.

The Ogress looked up at her and smiled. "Hello," she said with a smile that didn't reveal her fangs. Jenny looked at the desk found the name. Gia, there it was. "Hello, Gia. I need some supplies," Jenny said and sat down. "I assumed as much, details, case number, you know the routine," Gia replied more like a machine than anything.

"That's the thing. This is an SR twenty-two case, you know how it is," Jenny replied and Gia raised an eyebrow. "We don't get many of those types anymore. I guess it came straight from the boss. The less I know the better," Gia said and pulled out a blue sheet of paper from a drawer on the other side of the desk. She slid it to her. "Just sign here and I'll give you the code," Gia said and Jenny looked at the page, and the end of her career at the same time.

She picked up the pen and began to sign her name on the line. Gia shook her head a little bit. "There is something strange about you," she said and Jenny finished signing her name. "What do you mean strange?" Jenny asked, nervous all of the sudden. "You smell, no, not smell, feel familiar to me. No, not that either. You remind me of a different time," Gia replied to her and Jenny was not interested in sitting here much longer all of the sudden.

"You've been in the presence of Jorin, how is that possible?" she asked quietly, almost eager as her red eyes widened. Jenny didn't know what was going on. "The King, you know where he is, you have his energy all over you, I can feel it," she replied and Jenny rolled her eyes. "Listen, Jorin is dead. This has to be something weird. Maybe its just a weird—" Gia cut her off. "I served under the king in the war, kind of. Okay I saw him once at a troop rally, if he's alive you need to tell me, right now," she said with an intense glare in her eyes.

"Listen, Jorin's dead. We were on a case and we happened to find his heart in a metal box. Special Operations took over before we could do anything else. I don't know anything after that," Jenny said and Gia leaned back in her office chair with a smile. "I knew he wasn't dead, they can't destroy his heart and its only a matter of time before someone found him," she said and was full of energy. Even her Noxite was glowing a little brighter.

Jenny didn't even want to tell her anything close to the truth but hoped it might help her get away with this lie. "Anyway, can I have my code now?" she asked and Gia calmed down. "Sure, here it is," she said, pushed a button and a plastic, red card popped out of a slit on her desk. Jenny picked it up. "You've made my day, Pixie. Get out of here," Gia said and Jenny took the advice got up and left, she wasn't exactly sure if she did the right thing by telling the vampire anything at all.

Also, she was worried that now one knew the word would spread in a hurry. If Gia could detect the energy of the old king on her, all of them would. This was not something she was expecting. It would be a problem for later. Now she needed to get her supplies and get out of here before someone caught on to what was going on.

Cornell was flying through the shadow realm looking for something that could be used as a good enough transport. He had a place in mind to look first and it didn't take him long to find it. Lonnie Moreno, the prince dwip of Echemos was doing what he always did. Showing off what his father's money bought him this week. Usually something big, expensive and useless in a city. Cornell kept close track of everyone in the family and had done so for years. Anyone dumb enough to show off and be in the open.

Cornell landed on the roof of the restaurant his target was just pulling up to. Some fancy elf food place, strange because Lonnie was a Troll. Cornell watched as the troll prince got out of his oversized thing that was clearly not meant for city roads. Even if it was hovering a couple of feet off the ground Lonnie had no trouble at all getting out. Then on the other side two women got out. Both human and both of them dressed like they came right out of some brothel in Black Sand. Cornell figured they likely did.

Cornell didn't care who he was with, but it was strange he wasn't surrounded by guys with guns today. He supposed that the Troll was trying to impress the ladies or some dumb thing. There were plenty of people who wanted him dead.

"Only the best for you, ladies," Lonnie said and outstretched his arms. Cornell jumped off the roof and back into the physical realm just in time to land on the roof of the car. "Hey there, Lonnie," Cornell said and Lonnie turned to look. "No armed guards today, I'm impressed, or maybe daddy just figured you're not worth protection anymore," he finished saying to him. Lonnie snarled in response to that.

"You red freak. I didn't do anything wrong and you can't prove anything so get out of here before I rip you apart," he said and Cornell smiled. "Big words for such a little man," he said and jumped off the transport to the ground. "I'd skin you alive just to send a message to your dad that I'm never going away," Cornell said in his altered voice and Lonnie backed off a step. Stories of skinless criminals were not unheard of in Echemos.

"I'm going to borrow this transport, give me the keys and I won't break all of your bones. I'll even leave you in peace. How does that sound?" Cornell asked and Lonnie grunted. "You want these keys, you're going to have to come take them from me," he replied and Cornell smiled under his helmet, he was in a hurry, he didn't have time to follow through on either of the threats this time around.

Cornell jumped to the ground and rushed towards the troll and lunged forward. The troll threw a sloppy left hook at Cornell's head. He spun around and avoided the attack. At the same time, he grabbed the left arm with both hands. He pulled it straight back and the pain sent Lonnie forward putting his face into the pavement in seconds.

"Please, stop. I'll do anything," Lonnie begged as he was quickly overpowered. "Then scream," Cornell said as he pulled back on the arm and the sound of the snapping bone almost sounded like a gunshot. Lonnie screamed as Cornell picked up the keys. Then he looked at the women who watched the whole event in horror.

"This fancy thing here? It was all paid with blood money, drugs and general things that make most normal people scream in misery every day. Don't go home, and pray that the rest of his family doesn't come after you. Leave the city, lay low for a few weeks, if you value your lives at all anyway," he said to them and they ran off screaming. Cornell didn't know if any of that was true. When it came to embarrassing stories, well, the Moreno family didn't like those things to spread to the other syndicates in various places.

"As for you, Lonnie boy, thanks for your cooperation," he said and the troll just groaned in pain. "Tell your father he's next, along with the rest of your inbred, pathetic excuse for a family," Cornell said to him in a low voice. "I will, I'll tell him," he said and Cornell smashed his head against the ground, he thought about killing him but he was sure at least one person was watching by now and murder was still illegal in public, at least, so he just left him knocked out there in front of the restaurant.

Cornell put his hand on the transport. In seconds himself and the thing disappeared into the shadow realm. He got inside the thing and started it up. It must have been new because it still had that new car smell. "Lucky me," he said and piloted the thing into the air, now all he had to do was make his way back to the tower, in all, everything felt like it was getting off to a good start.

# Chapter Seventeen

Cornell made it back to the Tsuba building and materialized back into the real world. Jenny was waiting for him there and Zozo was there as well. "You go out to get a ride and this is what you get?" Zozo asked when he saw it and Cornell rolled down the window. "Yeah, I had to borrow it. Can we go now or do we have something to pick up yet?" he asked back, hoping Jenny was successful. Since she was here, he supposed everything went fine.

"We're good to go," Jenny asked and picked up the pack she got, holding out to show it off. Cornell was impressed because he knew what it was when he saw it. "Good, get up here so we can head out," Cornell replied and the two of them floated to the door as it slid open.

"This is nice," Jenny said as she got into the front seat. "Hey, I know where the place is, shouldn't I sit in the front?" Zozo complained and Cornell shook his head. "No," he said and as soon as the door closed, Cornell pulled away from the building and his armor disappeared. "Start talking," Cornell said but tried not to sound too annoyed yet. It could be a long trip.

"First we need to get over the Scorched wall, then I'll guide you from there," Zozo replied and leaned back into the seat that he thought was too soft. "Any particular direction or just a vague that way?" Cornell asked. "Trust me, it doesn't matter. Just get us over the wall," Zozo replied in annoyance. Cornell wondered what he meant by it didn't matter.

"Is he always like that?" Jenny asked. Cornell nodded. "Usually. I'm surprised he hasn't tried to kill us yet, personally," he replied, he was only half kidding about that too.

"I'm literally right here, guys," Zozo said and honestly right now was wondering if getting what he wanted was worth all this disrespect he was getting right now. Tiny sparks of flame danced around his fingers. For a second, he considered it, but the fire faded away. Maybe later he'd do it.

"Oh, I forgot about something," Jenny said and Cornell looked over. "What?" he asked and she shrugged. "I overheard something called the Cansema cult," she said, hoping it was important somehow. Cornell had heard of them before and nodded.

"Cansema cult, really? That's weird," Zozo replied. The conversation felt it like it was over, Cornell nodded and "Okay, I know I'm not in the superhero or villain club, but could someone please explain to me what that is?" she asked again refusing to just let it go.

"Oh right, villains. You know just because someone wants to try something new doesn't make them a bad guy, it usually makes them a visionary," Zozo replied. "Don't even start with that visionary crap again, if I have to hear that speech, I am going to stop this car and beat you so hard your parents can feel it," Cornell replied, his eyes widened with a quick fury.

Zozo just smiled and got to the point. "Cansema is the God of time, from what I understand. Like Delrax I guess, in a way. A group of necromancers claim to worship the three gods of evil. I mean, it seems kind of weird to call them such a generic name, but they do that. Also, they claim to know the secret history of the world," Zozo said as he stared down at the city below as they flew over it.

"No one has ever seen any evidence that any of these so called Gods exist, no blades, no temples, no nothing. Most people don't know the cult even exists," Cornell said and continued. "I've stumbled on some of their schemes quite by accident in the cities around Vanir. One time they wanted to poison the air, another time the just wanted to kill all the halflings. None of their plans made much sense," Cornell finished with a shrug. He was pretty sure if Cansema was the god of time, no one told that to his followers who always seemed insane to him.

"Three evil gods," Jenny said, talking to herself. "Eight gods aren't enough, we need three evil ones, too?" she asked. "Like your boyfriend said, no evidence of them even exists. The cults do, but they are mostly just drug addicts, crazy people and losers, and a few really high powered mages," Zozo replied. "The necromancers that worship them are on their own thing. Every god has their own special blend of crazy followers," Zozo finished, he knew a lot more than that, but it wouldn't help anyone to know any of it.

"Where we are going, we shouldn't have to worry about them, besides everyone here knows the vampire is responsible for what happened," Cornell said and Zozo just shrugged. "Speaking of going, don't you need to get the item?" Zozo asked. "No, don't do that oh Taro in all the stress of putting my career in the blender I forgot one more thing," Jenny replied at once. "What is it now, do you need a brain scan or something?" Zozo replied and Cornell just groaned at the comment, it was going to be like this the whole trip.

Jenny ignored the comment and kept going. "The vampire at the supply desk could sense the energy of the heart on me, just because I was close to it. If we have it out in the open it will likely attract all of them nearby. That could be bad because Gia seemed pretty excited about the idea of the old king returning," she said in a hurry.

"Wonderful, but no. I think its safe in the shadow realm for now. The alarm hasn't gone off and I can go get it when we get to the temple," Cornell replied. "It is interesting that vampires would be able to sense Jorin's energy over a hundred years later. I guess its true, vampire Kings are immortal," Zozo said as he looked out the window, seeing the city pass below them. It looked peaceful from up here, almost nice. "But doesn't that mean the vampire will know exactly where we are?" she asked and Zozo smiled. "Yes," he replied. Jenny tried to take her mind somewhere else.

"They hardly talked about the last war in school. Just that it formed the eight kingdoms we have today and the alliance won," Jenny said, now she wished she knew more about the past. "Public school systems are terrible. All I know is that if Jorin is brought back all hell could break loose," Zozo replied and smiled, he liked the idea, but didn't like the idea of such a powerful figure returning to the world. It would complicate his own plans.

The three of them traveled through the sky in silence for thirty more minutes, moving along at a good pace when in the distance, there it was. The wall looked like a long, black mountain stretching for as far as the eye could see in either direction.

"The Scorched wall protects all of Vanir from the Outside. I've never been past this wall before," Jenny said, then she wondered why the capital was this close to the wall in the first place. That didn't make much sense. "Yeah, I've been out here a couple times but not too far," Cornell replied. "I used to live out here. It's a fun place. Dragons, horrible golems and all kinds of monsters are out here. If we're lucky we won't meet any of them," Zozo replied.

"Dragons?" Cornell asked and Zozo nodded. "Yep, Dragons," he replied. Cornell had only heard about them, but like Unicorns, they were pretty rare to see. He kind of wanted to see one actually, but maybe from a distance. That would be just fine too.

The wall in the distance kept Jenny's attention, then something above it did too. "It's the guards," she said and pointed. In the sun they looked like tiny black dots, insects buzzing around over the top. "Alright guys, hold on," Cornell said and he grasped the mirror in his hand. It lit up and in seconds them and their flying car was transported into the shadow realm.

"Oh my god," Jenny said and didn't specify on which. The whole wall was a writhing mass of tentacles and beasts hooked to it and flying over it that changed shape as they sailed through the air Jenny averted her eyes in a hurry.

"The wall was built by the gods according to the legends, it radiates magical energy and the monsters here are attracted to it. Get ready to fight. Remember, any magical attacks are amplified in this realm, what might be average in our world could be a whole lot different here," Cornell said and his hands tightened on the steering wheel. He didn't want to get stopped by these things but a swarm would be hard to avoid entirely.

"Don't worry, go as fast as this thing can go, get over the wall and out of this dimension as soon as we can. We'll be fine as long as you don't screw up," Zozo replied and Cornell rolled his eyes, but didn't bother saying anything.

He pushed the thing as fast as he could go, the engine whined as the speed increased. Jenny closed her eyes, then a hand came down on her shoulder. "Don't close your eyes. We need to keep watch. I know, seeing this just isn't right and it's going to stick with you forever. But we are going to make it. These things are basically living darkness, we can handle it," Zozo said. It didn't make her feel any better, but he was right.

She looked out the window and did her best not to throw up or panic. Something about being here felt wrong. "Come on Cornell drive faster," she said as she became increasingly more worried about the situation they were in. "I am going as fast as I can, we'll be past it in just a few minutes at this rate," he replied, but mostly to himself as he focused on the task at hand.

Cornell wished this thing had weapons on it right now. He turned hard to the left and avoided a flying thing. As they flew past it, the thing seemed to be torn apart by the force, then reform. "Watch out," Zozo yelled but it was a few seconds too late.

Thick, black tentacles shot from the wall and wrapped around their car, stopping it cold in the air. "Damn it," Cornell said as he grit his teeth and did his best to pull away from the thing but it wasn't doing any good.

"Do something before it crushes us," Cornell yelled. "Fine," Zozo replied and rolled down the window. The thing smelled like sulfur and decay. Zozo's left hand lit on fire and he shot a deep blue flame out of the side window. The blast shredded the tentacle into nothing. Jenny rolled her window down and fired her own golden energy at approaching tendrils and the tentacles were blasted away but only to be replaced by several more. Jenny knew what needed to be done. "Be right back," she said as she shrank down to her normal size and shot out the open window without trying to think about it too much.

"Jenny, wait," Cornell said, but it was pointless. All he could do now was try his best not to be dragged down. He would have transformed but now he realized how much of a mistake it was for him to be the driver. "Detective, you should know better than to try to tell her what to do by now," Zozo said to him and laughed about it.

"Shut up, firebrand," Cornell replied as the whole car shook and started to get dragged towards the writhing mass below.

Jenny looked at the situation and saw the problem right away a thick stalk under the car had sprouted up and turned into lots of tentacles. It looked as if the whole thing was the worse half of a giant sand squid. "Okay," she said to herself and her hands lit up with white hot energy. She didn't think about the effects of the realm on her natural powers and fired.

Two white, thick hot beams of energy fired below the car. The light and shadows didn't mix very well. Jenny's power shredded the thickest piece of the living dark and all of the tentacles holding the car dissipated at once. "And that's how you get work done," she said with a smile. Her victory didn't last long as something from behind shrieked, it made her jump and spin around.

A formless black thing was flying in her direction, she still had no idea how the dark could just come to life but here it was, doing just that. "Damn you," she said and fired again. Her beam hit its mark and the thing was blasted into pieces, the pieces fell away as if they were nothing more than just ashes in the black and white surroundings. Jenny looked around and only saw more of these things coming in her direction, coming for them all. She flew back to the car and through the window. "Get the hell out of here already," she yelled and Cornell just shook his head.

"I didn't want to leave you behind," he replied and punched the accelerator. The transport jerked and flew forward. "I would have left you behind," Zozo said and Jenny didn't believe it for a second. The shadow creatures lashed out at them but Cornell dodged them with tight turns. Jenny wasn't strapped in and still tiny. She slammed into the window and heard something in her left arm snapped. She screamed, but to Zozo it sounded as if it were nothing more than air being let out of a tire.

Cornell watched as they passed over the infested wall and as soon as they were he pulled them all out of the shadow realm. The colors returned to the world at once and it didn't look like they were detected, no one was coming after them.

Jenny grew to her normal size in the front seat, holding her arm. "Are you okay?" Cornell asked. Jenny just groaned in response. "I'll fix her," Zozo replied. Cornell wanted to get farther away before he landed. "Fine, if she's fine with it then do it," Cornell replied.

"Well, are you fine with it or not?" Zozo asked and Jenny leaned back. The bone was sticking out of her arm an there was blood running down. "Sure, make it better," she said between breaths, in pain. She was in the back seat. Zozo smiled and put his hands on the wound. Jenny winced in pain. Then a golden light appeared from under his hands.

Jenny closed her eyes and in a few minutes her arm felt better. "Didn't know you knew how to heal," she said. "It's not something I advertise. Besides the smell of blood will attract all kinds of things out here. Better to just take care of it now," he replied and did his best not to look at her when he said it.

"Speaking of taking care of things, where do we go now?" Cornell asked and Zozo took his hands away from Jenny's arm. It was like it was before. "Loa's old temple is far from here. We need to get to the Blasted Sand," he said as if everyone knew where that was. "So, I don't take a lot of trips to the outside. Would you like to point in a general direction, maybe?" Cornell asked, getting annoyed. "Go West, the Blasted Sand is about as far west as you can go before you hit the water," Zozo replied.

"Westward bound then," Cornell said and turned the transport to the west. The sun was high in the sky now, the heat was starting to get to all of them. "How far is it?" Jenny asked.

"The western borders aren't far from here. How long it will take to get there is impossible to know," Zozo said and continued. "We might meet some unfriendly things along the way," he finished. Jenny looked out the window. The Scorched Wall was disappearing behind them and all that was visible now was endless sand. "If I live through this I am moving to the Western Kingdom. No more deserts ever again," she said, complaining.

"You sure like the extremes, don't you?" Zozo asked. "Hell, I don't know. Right now, anywhere seems like a better choice than out here," she said and all the sudden started to feel a sense of dread come over here. All of the stories she'd ever heard about this place started coming back to her. All the creatures that supposedly lived out here, and things that were never alive stalked the place.

"Creepy, isn't it?" Cornell asked. "Nothing but us for miles," he said with a laugh. "Don't fool yourself, we're not alone out here," Zozo replied to him as he looked out into the sand as they passed over it.

# Chapter Eighteen

The transport coasted over the sand, the three passengers were busy doing their best to make sure nothing was coming after them. For the first hour everything was quiet. "So, a century ago. Did people really fight and die over all this sand?" Jenny asked. Zozo nodded. "Yeah, all over the world they fought in the Outside. It was a big ordeal, but we should focus on the swirling column of sand behind us," Zozo said a little too casually.

Jenny looked and sure enough it was a twisting, tall and horrible line of sand that seemed to be alive as it chased them down. "What is it?" she asked, swearing that she could see eyes in the storm, if that's what it was.

"The old nomads call them Jinn, some call them Genies, others think they are just air elementals that went insane," Zozo said with a shrug. "Who cares what it is, how do we lose it?" Cornell asked. "I don't know. Sometimes they just give up, sometimes we have to kill it. Maybe we can bribe it. Have any red, shiny artifacts you want to give away. That might work," he replied. Cornell rolled his eyes at the suggestion.

"Kill an elemental, that's possible?" Jenny asked. "Sure is, it just takes some work, whatever we plan to do, lets go ahead and do it?" Zozo asked again as the thing got closer.

"We could go into the shadow realm," Cornell suggested. "No, giants live out here in that realm. They'd be on us in a second.

We really should only go there as a last resort," Zozo said and looked out the back window. "Well, Jenny, you drive. I'll take care of this thing and catch up. Hurt her and I'll make you wish you were dead, I promise," Cornell said to both of them, opened the door. He climbed out of the transport and clung to the side.

Then as he leapt out of the thing he transformed into his armor as he hit the sand and stood up. The whirling column of sand stopped. Cornell watched the thing shrink down and quickly take the form of a humanoid shape. "Wonderful," he said to himself.

"Hey, wind guy. Would you mind not chasing us down, that's just not too cool," Cornell said, not really knowing what else to say. "You trespass," it said, but it's voice just sounded like the wind blowing through invisible trees.

"Just passing through, we don't want to take anything, I promise. Once we're done we'll go back home," Cornell said and the wind figure stood there for second, thinking, maybe. "You will be scattered," the thing replied to him. "Yeah I thought you might say that," Cornell replied and prepared for a fight. It would be the first time he'd ever fought a living sandstorm before, and he wasn't looking forward to the experience.

The elemental outstretched its arms and sand in its body turned its arms into long curved blades, then without missing a beat the thing lunged forward. Cornell didn't want to take chances that his armor could take the hit or not and flew into the sky.

"My sky, you will die," the thing said in a broken screech as it spun around and blasted sand in his direction. He wasn't fast enough to avoid it. The sand blasted him and knocked him out of the sky on impact. It was as if he was being hit by a thousand pounds of liquid cement. It knocked the wind out of him as he hit the ground sending the red sand in all directions.

Cornell coughed trying to catch his breath, he swore that he could feel sand in his armor already, but it was just his imagination, he hoped at least. He picked himself up out of the sand and tried to think of what to do next. This thing had to have a weakness of some kind but right now wasn't the best time to stop and think. The living sandstorm started to do what it was good at. Instead of remaining in a human form, the thing exploded back into the storm it was.

Now the only thing Cornell could see was the darkness of blowing sand and hear the howling of the unnatural winds around him. He closed his eyes and did his best to think. Necromancer training served him well in the past, and he needed to remember the things he learned.

"Where's your heart?" he whispered to himself. All elementals had a heart of kind, or a core. Whatever, it was all the same. He focused his senses and tapped into his armor's power. There it was. The second he saw it dimly with his other sight, the wind blew him up from the ground and a tendril of sand wrapped around his neck and pulled him farther up into the air.

"Die, flesh thing," a voice said to him from all directions. There was no reasoning with the madness of the elemental, that was clear. Cornell didn't want to use any of his power against this thing, not more than he needed to at least. He clenched his left fist and threw it up through the tendril of sand, shattering it, he didn't fall to the ground, however.

Cornell shot straight up into the air, out of the living storm and turned around. The mass lunged straight for him, just like he knew it would. "Powerful, but stupid," Cornell said to himself and dived straight back in to the thing as fast as he could. The core of the beast was beginning to shine in his vision the more he focused on it. It was tiny, half the size of a tin can.

He tore through the sand as fast as he could. Reaching out he snatched the heart of the thing in his right hand as he fell to the ground. It burned hot, even through his armor. The sand immediately fell to into the desert. "Okay you old windbag, you've pissed me off for the last time," Cornell said and started to squeeze the clear crystal.

"No, mercy," a voice whispered on the winds, weaker now, in agony. "Oh, now you want mercy. Now you want a break after trying to grind me to dust?" Cornell asked the invisible thing, holding its heart in his hand. "Please," it whispered again. Cornell couldn't even imagine how many people it's killed over the centuries.

"And if I do, you promise to never come after anyone ever again?" Cornell asked and there was no response. "Well?" he asked again. "Yes, promise," it replied. "Good," Cornell replied and tossed the elemental heart into the sky. At once a column of wind shot past him and stole it away. He watched as the sandstorm swirled away from him and disappear in the distance. With that he took off into the sky and hoped he could pick up the trail of the transport. There couldn't have been too many things moving out here at a high rate of speed.

Soon enough he found the trail left in the sand. He shot off into the distance and it didn't take him long to find the transport. To his dismay, it had stopped beside what looked like a tower and it was clearly very old.

"What in the hell is going on?" he asked himself and flew down to the transport. No one was inside. Two sets of tracks lead straight to the building. The door at the base of the tower was open. Cornell knew that what ever was going on here, it couldn't have been good.

He walked inside quickly, and the second he did he was greeted with an impossible stairway. It looked like it went up hundreds of feet above the outside of the tower itself. He took off straight up into the tower. The staircase spiraled around him and all of this was strange. He knew that he had left them behind, but would they really have enough time to make it all this way up, sure they could have flown, he supposed, but why?

Cornell blasted up as fast as he could, at the top of the tower was a dried out, black and wooden door. There was only one place they could be. He floated to the ledge and pushed the door open. "Don't worry, Pixie, your sacrifice won't be in vain," Zozo said as he walked past. Jenny was strapped to a table with a large purple crystal hanging over head beginning to glow.

"I can't leave you alone for a second, can I?" Cornell asked and Zozo turned around. "He's crazy, let me out of here, now," Jenny said and tried to struggle. Something was preventing her from using her natural powers.

"This is what I need. This is going to fix the whole world. I just need to do a few more things and your partner here is going to be a whole new woman," Zozo replied, almost manically. Cornell looked around and didn't see anything here but the crystal above them. No books. No science equipment, nothing useful.

"Zozo listen to me. This isn't what you think, this is a prison tower," Cornell said, he'd seen this kind of crystal before, although never so big. "What do you mean prison tower, this is the lab of the ancients. I can finally complete my experiments here. You'll see," he replied almost manically. "Damn it," Cornell replied and walked to Jenny's table. He started to free her when Zozo turned around and cleared the distance between them.

Zozo grabbed Cornell by the throat, picked him up with ease and tossed him back into the wall. He hit so hard the ancient stone wall cracked on impact. "No, you won't stop me again," he screamed at him with a growing insanity.

"There is nothing to stop you idiot, none of this is real," Cornell yelled back, got up and knew that he wasn't in his right mind, but he couldn't hurt him either. He was the only one who knew where the temple was.

"You're the crazy one Mirror. I will kill her right now if you interfere again. Finding subjects is easy enough," he replied at a manic pace. There was only one thing left to do about any of this. Cornell raised his hands and fired deep red beams of light at the crystal. The thing swung on impact, was blasted off of its chain and into the wall, shattering into countless pieces. Wasting no time, he rushed to Jenny's side and his cape of pure red energy appeared over the both of them.

The pieces shattered into nothing on impact and in just a few seconds the whole ordeal was over. Then it was quiet. Zozo was staring at a stone wall, dazed. "What in the hell just happened?" he asked and shook his head. Then he picked up a tiny shard of the purple crystal. "Joxhorn Crystal," he said and flicked it to the floor.

Cornell freed Jenny with ease. "Are you happy now, Zozo, how did you fall for any of this?" he asked with anger. "No, I heard it from in the tower. The hum of machinery, science, magic. This cursed crystal is bigger than any I've ever seen before. No wonder it lured me inside," he replied and looked towards him. "I'm sorry," Zozo replied and Cornell didn't quite know what to say.

"Fine, whatever, lets just get out of here before you decide you want to fight to the death or something else equally bad," Cornell said and helped Jenny up, making sure she wasn't impaled anywhere. "I'm fine, back off, thanks for the save, but I'm fine," she said and got off the table. "Just making sure," he replied and stood back. He wondered what the Joxhorn crystal made her see to come inside this place. He didn't want to dwell on it anymore.

"Yeah, lets get out of here," Zozo said and the three of them headed back through the door. Instead of being a long trip up it was just a few steps outside, back into the heat and the sand. "I really hate Joxhorn crystals," Cornell said and looked back towards the tower. The place, the purpose and who built it. None of them would ever know what it was. Maybe it was best that way. "Come on, lets go," Jenny said and walked to the transport and got inside.

"Where are we going now?" Cornell asked as he got in the drivers' side. "Keep going in the same direction," Zozo said as he got inside and closed the door. The second everyone was inside, Cornell pulled away from the mysterious tower.

# Chapter Nineteen

The desert was unchanging as they flew over the dead sand. "You know, at the risk of sounding annoying. You said it wasn't far away from here and we've been driving for hours now. So, are we there yet?" Jenny asked.

"No," Zozo replied and stared out the window. "Well, if not, we have to consider our situation," Cornell said. "As soon as that sun is gone a nasty elder vampire is going to be coming right in our direction, we need a plan," he said and Jenny just shrugged. "Why don't we just kill her? We have you, me and this guy. I think we could take her if we prepared," she said, still trying to put the events of a few hours ago behind her.

"Pixie has a point, why don't we just deal with it and not worry about being chased?" Zozo agreed with her. Cornell didn't like the idea. "That's a great plan, but we are outside. There is no telling just how many creatures she would have gotten under her control. It's been a fair amount of time. Do you really want to wait and find out what she has in tow?" he asked them. Zozo just shrugged. "I don't care if the vampire has a whole army. I still think we can win," he replied.

Cornell didn't know what to do, but he did know that the sun was going to be down soon and in the dark, a vampire wouldn't be their only problem out here.

"Well whatever we decide to do, let me know. I'm cool either way," Jenny said then Cornell stopped the transport. "What in the hell is that?" he asked and they all looked out the front window together. In front of them was what looked to be a statue of a man who was desperately was trying to get away from something made out of black stone.

"Looks like a statue to me," Zozo said. "I know what it looks like, but what is it doing here, you know, the obvious questions that come to mind," Cornell replied to him, annoyed with him. "Look, over there," Jenny pointed and there was another one in a similar fashion. A black rock statue of a woman, trying to get away from something.

Cornell pulled forward slowly and on the other side of a sand dune, there was a whole collection of about fifty more black stone statues. "What is this?" he asked quietly. "Looks like more statues," Zozo replied and Cornell was just about ready to hit him in the face. Zozo just smiled.

"Seriously, it looks like a Dead Eye Cyclops or maybe a Black Gorgon lives around here. All the victims could have been ones who were unlucky enough to crash out here on an air ship, then something found them. Chances are its still here somewhere. So, I suggest we not be here, maybe?" Zozo asked, not caring what made it and was just hoping not to meet it.

"I like that idea, let's get out of here before we find out what did this," Jenny agreed with that idea. Cornell did too and began to look for a clear path in how to get around the morbid stone collection that was in front of them.

The three of them went quiet as they slowly went around them. They all were all mostly in one place, as if what ever got them did it mostly at the same time. As they moved around, there was the source of the people. It was a sand covered, broken silver airship. In bright yellow letter there on the side of the thing was the name 'Silver Sky.'

"Wow, I remember hearing about this a few years ago. They never found it," Jenny said and Zozo rolled his eyes. "No, they found it. They just didn't want anyone coming out to look for it. That's what you do when airships go missing and you run into this. You cover it up and hope the sand takes it before anyone else sees it," Zozo said and Jenny hated to think that was true.

"There isn't anything we can do for them now, we need to keep going," Cornell replied and kept going. As they went along the edge of the statues. Jenny saw a hole in the side of the ship, in the darkness she swore that she could see scales just barely glinting off the sunlight on the inside. It could have been anything, however. It was about now she wished that he would drive a little faster.

"There's the beast," Zozo said, confirming what she had seen. Cornell wasn't worried about the things he could see, he didn't want to punch it and run into a hidden statue turning their ride into a wreck.

"Well as long as it stays over there we'll be fine," Cornell said. If you weren't a little bit scared being out here, you had to be insane, he thought. The last thing he wanted to do was face down a beast from the outside for any reason. He was surprised the engine noise wasn't making it attack. Of course, it could have been dead too. There was no way to tell from here and that was fine with him.

"I sure hope so," Jenny whispered. Something about this whole scene was making her deeply unsettled. She had seen so many criminal acts, vicious things but never anything quite like this. Something about the frozen terror on the faces all these people had was going to give her nightmares, she just knew it.

"Cornell, these people deserve to be avenged. No one asked to be turned into a statue like this," Jenny said and it came out of nowhere. "Maybe we can do it on the way back, right now we need to get to the Loa's temple so we can do what we came out here for," he replied just as fast. He wasn't in the business of fighting actual monsters. He felt bad, sure, but not that bad.

"Avenged? No, that's just the bad luck of the draw. Anyone who crosses the distance between kingdoms know what the risk is. They didn't deserve it, it was just bad luck. Besides if you kill the beast, what if the spell breaks? Then you have who knows how many people who are supposed to be dead wandering around a desert. No one will rescue them because that would look bad for the company and we can't do much to help. Also, they could all be dead anyway, there is no way to tell. They are better off right where they are," Zozo replied and Jenny wanted to hit him, but then she supposed he had a point.

"Fine, let's put some distance between us and this place," she said quietly, frustrated about the whole situation as they left it behind. "I'll report it to Mystic Headquarters when we get back so we can do something about it then," Cornell said, he knew she would do it anyway so he decided to do his best to make her feel better.

A hideous roar overcame the silence behind them as they began to climb the next dune. "Oh, come on, we were almost out," Cornell complained as he heard it. "No point in being quiet now, punch it Red," Zozo yelled and looked behind them.

There it was, the Black Gorgon just as he thought. It was all reptile with the top half of the thing resembling a woman and the end was the tail of a long snake. However, the top half was covered in black scales as well. The creature shot out of its lair and had to be at least fifteen feet tall. "She's chasing us, Red you need to hurry," Zozo said, trying to be calm.

"I am going as fast as this thing can, I think," he replied but the Gorgon was still catching up. "Fine. I'll distract it this time, you got the last one," he said, opened the door and jumped out. "Damn it man wait," Cornell replied seconds too late.

"We have to help him," Jenny said and Cornell knew she was right. He was the only one who knew where the temple was and without him, the whole mission was lost. Cornell slammed on the brakes and the hovering transport came to a stop and landed on the ground with a soft thud.

Zozo flew through the air and shot a cone of black flame into the monster's face, she screamed in pain as the black flames clung to her face and chest. "Now you face me, you are going to regret trying to add to your collection today, snake," he said and wasn't entirely sure why, the Gorgon likely couldn't understand him anyway.

However, stories existed in the ancient texts that claim the Gorgons used to be their own race, and have their own kingdom. The information was scarce and no one knew if it was true or not. So, maybe it could understand him. He wasn't sure. If it could, she wasn't showing it.

The black flames quickly died out and didn't do any damage to the thing. It did anger her on the other hand. Zozo dived out of the way with the beast's eyes fired twin, bright yellow rays of light. The rays hit the sand and the sand turned into slabs of black stone immediately. Zozo slid in the sand backwards and slammed his left foot into it as he came to a stop. Columns of more black fire exploded all around the beast, creating a cage of fire.

The Gorgon swiped at the flames only for them to reform. "That should hold you for a minute. Now to get back to the," he stopped as he saw Cornell and Jenny coming his way. "So much for believing in me," he said to himself. "Guys get back to the transport, we're done here," Zozo yelled. The two of them stopped in their tracks seeing the cage of fire holding it back.

"Guess he didn't need help after all," Cornell said and started to turn back. The Gorgon roared at the two of them and fired her yellow beams at them. Cornell dived out of the way. Jenny was transfixed by the intense color of the beams and failed to move. Jenny was instantly turned to a black rock sculpture on contact.

"No," Cornell yelled as he watched his partner get petrified. Zozo was watching too and now there was only one choice left. "We have to kill it," Zozo said to him as he ran over to him. "Are we sure that will even work and what about all the others?" Cornell asked. "I don't know anything, but it's literally the only thing we can try right now," he replied in a hurry.

Cornell grabbed his mirror from his pocket and instantly transformed into his armored form. "Well then let's kill us a monster," Cornell said. "Hey, don't get stoned," Zozo replied and Cornell laughed a little bit before the both of them took to the air.

The black flame cage disappeared as soon as they flew. Cornell had never seen one of these things before and he wasn't exactly sure on how to kill one. He supposed it was the same way as you killed anything else. The Gorgon shot forward and, in her fury, she began to fire those beams at the both of them but they were too fast to be hit.

"You're the killer, any ideas on how to deal with snake lady down there?" Cornell asked and Zozo's golden eyes flared. "You take the head and I'll go low. Don't hold back and we should be fine," he replied and Cornell didn't know what to make of that or why he had to get the most dangerous part, but it didn't matter. "Hey, don't look at me like that, its your girlfriend, you stopped the transport you get the eyes," Zozo said to him again as if he could see through the helmet.

"Fine," Cornell said and the two of them split up. Zozo flew low and the Gorgon blasted her rays just behind him. Cornell's armor exploded with crackling red energy as she fired. He shot through the air as fast as he could and slammed his right fist into the side of her head knocking her into the sand. Cornell rarely had to push his armor's power to any kind of limits. The most he ever dealt with was the criminal scum of the underworld and they usually didn't have any powers he had to worry about.

The Gorgon grumbled in pain as it righted itself slowly only to get a stream of black fire slammed into her stomach. The pain made her screech and she slithered through the sand faster than Zozo could track with his eyes and she snatched him up with her right hand. "Red, now's the time," Zozo yelled out as the thing attempted to crush him.

Cornell blasted forward. The Gorgon fired her beams at him and he didn't have time to move. He crossed his arms without thinking about it. Then something he did not expect happened. The beams reflected off of his armor and hit the Gorgon in the face.

"They are magical in nature?" Cornell asked as he removed his arms to looks at what had happened. The Gorgon's head had been turned to stone instantly. Zozo was easily able to free himself then. "Did you know it was magical?" Cornell asked. "I had my suspicions, but no. I didn't know for sure. Your most annoying power turned out to be useful at last, go figure," Zozo replied to him.

The both of them turned to Jenny. The stone coating around her was beginning to dissolve in a black smoke around her. Then they turned to look at the others, the same thing was happening. However, these people had been imprisoned in stone too long. As the stone coating disappeared, their bodies began to fall to the ground, it was clear they were long dead by now. There was no possible way to save any of them.

Cornell flew back down to Jenny and caught her as she fell. She was gasping for breath. "Not statues," she managed to say as she coughed in pain. "Yeah, I see that. Come on, let's get out of here," he replied, picked her up and flew back towards the transport. Zozo looked at the sand field full of dead bodies and truly wondered If a Gorgon's magic would be enough to kill itself or not. He figured that if it was, it would be pretty big design flaw.

Zozo was just about to fly away when he noticed the stone surrounding the Gorgon's head begin to crack slightly. He didn't want to stick around anymore to find out what was going to happen so he turned around and followed the other two back to the car.

"It was horrible," Jenny said still trying to get over the thought of being covered in stone. "Yeah, that sucks but you're okay now," Cornell said as he landed next to the car. "Alright, get in," he said and let her down. Jenny climbed in the back seat and just laid across the back seat.

Zozo landed a few seconds later. "Looks like I get shotgun," he said and walked to the passenger side and got in. "Yeah I guess so," Cornell said to himself. Just then from just on the other side of the sand dune the familiar roar of the Gorgon sounded through the air. "Okay I don't want to do that again, lets get the hell out of here," Cornell said, deactivated his armor and quickly moved to the other side of the car, got in and started to drive away.

"With any luck she won't want to mess with us again," he said as the pulled away from the area. "I think a taste of her own medicine convinced her that maybe once was enough," Zozo replied. Cornell was glad he didn't have to actually kill the thing to save her.

"Alright, start talking. Where is this place. The sun is starting to set and we don't have much time," he said with a growing amount of anxiety in his voice. Zozo pointed to the west. Do you see that black patch of sand that looks like a line growing on the horizon there? That's it. The temple is in the middle of that place but even when you get there you can't just go inside. Loa wouldn't make it that easy, it took me years to figure out how to get down there, and you, well you get to do it on your first day so consider yourself lucky," Zozo replied to him annoyed at the situation.

"So, we're almost there then, great," Cornell replied, ignoring the subtext. "Yes, we're almost there," Zozo replied and looked out the window rolling his eyes.

# Chapter Twenty

The sun was shining right in their faces now, it was hard to see anything as they drove forward towards the black sand. It was only going to last just a bit longer and soon their real problems would begin. "Oh, there is something I should mention about the Blasted Sand," Zozo said after a period of silence.

"What's that?" he asked. "Electronics don't work there," he said casually. "What?" Cornell asked and continued. "You couldn't have mentioned this sooner?" Cornell asked, irritated. "Nope, I guess I forgot. It's been a few years. You forget things," he replied. Cornell realized that none of them had eaten or drank anything in hours and if it continued any more like this they would be killing one another soon.

He stopped the transport. "We have some natural light left. Now is a good time to get something to eat and stuff. We need a break," Cornell said and Zozo rolled his eyes. "Oh, Mister we need to never stop moving, now wants to relax, well, whatever. It sounds good to me, too," he replied, trying to be too irritated at the situation.

"Jenny, you awake back there?" Cornell asked as he came to a stop. "Yeah, a little bit," she replied and sat up. She was still extremely stiff and everything hurt on the inside. "We're gonna stop and eat, stuff like that. You have the supplies, right?" he asked and Jenny nodded. "Yeah I got it," she said and reached into her pocket and pulled out the golden card.

"This looks like a nice spot," Zozo said, but at the same time it all looked the same to Cornell, nothing but empty desert for miles. "Yeah sure, nice place," he replied and opened the door, got out. It was dead silent out here as always, and hot. Jenny and Zozo both got out at the same time.

Jenny swiped left across the golden card and three brown cloth packs appeared, hovered in the air. "There, one for each of us. I'm not entirely sure what is in each of these things but surprises make life worth living," she said with a forced smile. They each grabbed one and pulled it towards them. Once they did what ever magic that was keeping them in the air disappeared.

One by one they opened their packs and it was all the same things. A bottle of water, two meat sandwiches, a bar of chocolate and small bag of chips. "Oh boy, my favorite. Placement school packed lunches just like mom used to make," Zozo said and rolled his eyes. "It's better than starving to death out here so be grateful," Cornell said as he tore open the wrappings the sandwiches were in, the other two did the same.

The three of them ate in silence. Keeping an eye on their surroundings. They were sure they weren't the only hungry things out here and the smell of food might attract something else. Half way into the meal. "You know, we should have just eaten in the car," Jenny said as an offhand thought. "Yeah that would have been a great idea but I think stretching our legs out a bit isn't such a bad idea either," Zozo said with a shrug.

Jenny pulled the card out again and swiped it the other direction. Two small structures appeared. "Don't know about you guys but I got to go to the bathroom," she said and walked forward. "You detectives get all the coolest things," Zozo said and was being honest, he was impressed by that.

"Yeah, we do," Cornell gloated a little bit and walked in the other side. Zozo was alone. "I guess they trusted me to not kill them both," he said to himself and he was really tempted to burn them both alive, but resisted it. He wanted his book, he'd kill them after he got it. He figured that'd be fine.

Zozo looked up into the darkening sky and wondered just how eager they were to travel the Blasted sand on foot, or even in the air. There were lots of dangerous things out here at night. Just then Jenny came walking out.

"Well I feel better," she said and looked at him. "I was sure you were going to kill us all," she said and he shrugged. "I thought about it, but we're not at end of the deal so I decided not to. If I would have just killed you there would be no way Mr. Mirror in there would never agree to help me out. That much is clear," he replied and shrugged.

"See, you're not that crazy," she replied with a smile. "I guess not," he replied. Cornell came walking out and he sighed.

"Well, are we ready to go now or not?" he asked and they both nodded. "Are we really going into the area at night? Vampires aren't the worst of our problems out here," Zozo said and Cornell shook his head. "Yeah, we need to get there as soon as we can. See, its still barely sunny out here, back home the sun is down. She's already on her way here, now," Cornell said and Zozo shrugged. "Alright, you're the boss for now. Let's go," he replied.

Jenny swiped again on that golden card and everything it made appear, disappeared in an instant. "This thing is amazing, too bad I can't keep it," she said as she walked back to the car. "Why not?" Zozo asked as he followed. "Well, rules and stuff I guess," she replied and he laughed. "Screw the damn rules. You think rules got us this car? No way. Your boyfriend here stole it, I'm sure of it," Zozo replied.

"Yeah, but to be fair I did steal it from a criminal family who paid for it with drug money, and who knows what else. Hell, they likely just stole it from someone else as a debt payment," Cornell replied as they got inside.

"Well, I had to lie to get this card. I am sure by now everyone is looking for us," Jenny replied and continued. "Once they find us it'll be lucky if I just get fired for what I did for this mission," she finished and Zozo just smiled. "We're all criminals now, how's it feel?" he asked them. Cornell shrugged. "Bad guys don't have any rules, why should we?" he asked and smiled. "I can't wait to go to jail, it's going to be great fun," Jenny replied as she put the card away.

"Excellent, lets get out of here. The final destination awaits," he said and right now Zozo appeared to be the only happy person in the car, he was fine with that.

The three of them drove into the sunset. When the last few rays of the sun were gone, the car sputtered and died. "What in the hell is going on now?" Jenny asked and Zozo looked out the dark window. "We're here. This is as far as we go by car. No electronics allowed on the Blasted sand. We fly from here. So, do your best to be quiet. I came here the first time with twelve people. Only two of us made it out," Zozo replied and trailed off.

"Well, we'll be fine, come on, let's get this over with," Jenny replied, tried to be optimistic here in the face of the unknown.

"Yeah, just fine," Cornell replied but not quite sure if he actually believed that. The three of them got out of their car that had taken them this far and abandoned it. Cornell transformed into his armored form as they took to the skies above. Zozo lead the way in the dark. "Don't lose one another in the dark. Stay close and for damn sure don't listen to the noises and go to investigate them, please," Zozo warned and sent three bright pink sparks from his fingers.

"Identification fire spell. Only we can see it," he said to them as the flames wrapped around their left wrists like bracelets.

Jenny liked the way it looked, Cornell didn't trust it for a second but didn't worry about it too much yet.

In the dark, this section of the world didn't look like much of anything at all without any moonlight. Zozo and the others flew in what had to be a dead world. Cornell was beginning to think that all the horror stories of this place must have died out since the last time that he was here. Jenny thought she could hear someone screaming for help distance, or something that sounded like it. She knew better than to veer off into the dark, however and stayed with the others.

Then Zozo stopped in midair. Before anyone could ask why he raised his right hand, and hoped that they got the clue to be quiet. Thankfully they did. Zozo pointed to the left and flew that way and pressed up against rock. The other two followed him but didn't know why.

"What are we doing," Jenny whispered. "I don't know," Cornell replied. Zozo didn't say a word, but his eyes were focused on the darkness in front of them. It was clear that he knew something they didn't and right now there was no choice but to trust him right now.

Then, the darkness moved and thunder came from the ground. Even in the dark, something was there and it was massive. Zozo waved his hand slightly and a green bubble wrapped around the three of them. Now they could see in the dark, they could see that thing before them.

"Moro, Loa's pet as far as I can tell," Zozo whispered to them. The beast was hundreds of feet tall as it lumbered past them, at this range it looked like a wingless, bipedal dragon. It was impossible to tell what color the thing was because everything was a shade of green now. Even though they could see it, its face was still hidden in shadow. Only one red burning eye could be seen far above them.

"Wow, that's a pet?" Jenny asked as it moved past them. "Yeah, it's a pet, one of the biggest fire dragons I've ever seen," Zozo replied as the thing lumbered past them. "It could wipe any kingdom off the map," Jenny said without thinking.

"Yeah, I think it could too, but it sticks around here because the temple is here and like any good dog, it sticks around where its owner was last seen. It gives you a new respect for the power of the Gods doesn't it?" Zozo said and pulled himself off the wall. "Come on, if we're quiet she won't even know we're here," he said and the others followed him into the dark.

# Chapter Twenty-One

The moon rose over the desert revealing the landscape. It was sparkling from up here. The moonlight was reflecting off of something in the sand and it looked like gazing into an endless sea of stars.

"I know it looks great from up here but its just glass," Zozo said as he noticed she wasn't paying attention to where she was going. Jenny looked at him and was confused. "Yeah, this place, this whole desert is filled with thousands of years of history, I could spend countless lifetimes out here trying to learn it all," Zozo replied and smiled as he said it. She was about to say something when Cornell started to talk.

"Alright, professor, where is this temple, we must be close by now," Cornell said, tired of all the small talk and he didn't want Zozo getting in her head any more than he was trying to do, but he tried not to act so obvious.

"My red friend this whole place is her temple, it stretches from where we went in all the way to the ocean. It's vast, that's the secret no one realized, I didn't realize the first time. I was looking for a typical building, you know. A temple like you see in the movies. I know where the entrance is but it's going to take some work getting inside," Zozo replied to him.

That didn't really didn't tell him anything. Cornell couldn't help but feel that there was a particularly angry vampire that was closing in on them at a high rate of speed.

"What do you mean some work?" Jenny asked him, not liking the sound of that. "Fire golems guard the entrance. Two of them that burn with Loa's cosmic fire. We wrecked them the first time but they regenerate themselves so be ready for a fight," Zozo replied to her and smiled.

"Wonderful," she replied, disheartened at the thought of having to get into yet another fight in the wasteland, hopefully this time she'd fare a little better than before. She still shuddered at the thought of facing the Gorgon and being turned into a half statue.

"It won't be long now," Zozo replied to her and they pulled ahead of them to lead the way. "Is it just me or does it feel like we are being followed by something?" Cornell asked them, he couldn't help but feeling stalked right now.

"Likely lots of things are watching us right now. Lots of hungry things wondering If we're worth attacking or not. Everything is life and death out here and every move is made very carefully by predator and prey alike. So yes, Red, we are being followed. Ignore it and keep moving. If you slow down or stop you will make up their mind for them," Zozo replied to him, annoyed.

"Fine," Cornell replied, but he was sure their stalker was more than just wildlife, but for now he wouldn't mention it again just incase his imagination was running away from him. At this point, he had learned to trust his instincts.

The trio flew through the night, surrounded by hideous sounds in the distance, and some not so far away. Zozo didn't seem concerned by any of them and Cornell was doing his best to follow his lead, as much as he hated doing it. Jenny didn't like any of the noises either and was doing her best to imagine being back at home after all of whatever this was came to an end. She was also doing her best not to think about finding a new job or going to jail.

"Something's not right," Zozo said and stopped in midair. "What, besides being in a desert wasteland at night where everything is considering eating us, what else could be wrong?" Cornell asked and Zozo pointed at the ground. "We're at the entrance but the golems are destroyed. Look for yourself," he said.

The three of them looked and sure enough there were pieces of golem strewn about the place dying flames in the sand.

"Glad to see you could make it, I was wondering when you were going to show up," a voice called out from the dark. It was a voice Cornell knew all too well. "Damn it, we're too late," Cornell said and prepared for a fight.

"Where are you hiding come on out so I can get a good look at you," Zozo said and crossed his arms. She stepped out of the dark into the pale moonlight. Her eyes were just as bright blue as Cornell remembered them being.

"Professor Zozo, leader of the Firewalkers, right? Tell you what, if you kill those two, or help me do it. I'll help you get whatever they used as bait to get you to lead them here," she said with a smile.

"You can't do that, you know if that thing is brought back, we're all dead. Your book won't mean anything. Do you really want to be a food source for the vampires, really?" Cornell asked him. "Shut up, I'm thinking," Zozo replied. On one hand he really wanted to kill Cornell. On the other another war with the vampire race didn't feel like a good idea.

"Sorry, Red here has a good point. You just want to turn everyone into food and even I have higher standards than that. Besides, I'll kill these two in a way I want to, now just isn't that time, you're out of luck," Zozo said and didn't like saying that, but it was the best choice.

"If you want to die with them that's fine. You and the pixie I don't need. All I want is the Mirror," she said with a smile, then she began to levitate off the ground. "Yep, I always wanted to fight a pissed off elder vampire at night. It was one of my life goals," Jenny said and Zozo smiled at her sarcasm. "Just remember to cover your neck," he said and almost laughed about it.

Cornell didn't waste a second of time to go on the attack. He burned through the air as fast as he could and tackled the vampire right back to the ground. "What are you doing?" Jenny only had time to ask but by the time she did, the whole event was long since over.

"You guy friend here is an idiot, I guess," Zozo replied and smiled. "I could have torched her from here," he finished and she just shook her head in frustration. Because of the dust and the dark there was literally no way to tell what was going on down there. "You don't think she brought any friends, do you?" Jenny asked and Zozo was sure that a vampire like this didn't travel alone, but it was hard telling just what was lurking in the dark around them.

It was then Cornell came flying out of the dark and slammed into a stone column, the thing shattered under the force of the impact and toppled on top of him. Jenny was going to fly down and help but Zozo stopped her. "We don't have magic armor to protect us, let's get out of here so he doesn't have to worry if we're okay or not. Fly up," he said and honestly didn't care if she listened or not. He took off into the sky, away from the fight.

"You're useless Zozo," she yelled back, knowing he valued himself over anything else. She down to help Cornell in his fight. The vampire walked out of the dark and noticed her coming down and she smiled. "Perfect," she said to herself.

"No, run," Cornell yelled as he tossed a giant boulder off of him. Jenny realized that maybe Zozo was right to get away. Jenny tried to do the same but the vampire was too fast. Nearly instantly Jenny was seized, spun around like a rag doll to face Cornell. "One step further and she'll be drained so fast it might make your head spin," she said with a smile. "Or you can get the heart like I asked, give it to me and we can go our separate ways. Interested in that or are you just going to risk it?" she asked.

"Velima, please. I know you're obsessed with this heart, the past and all the other things. But it's a different world now. Please don't eat me because you can't let it go," Jenny said and the vampire paused. "How do you know my name?" she asked. "I'm a detective, Elder Vampires like yourself tend to be rare so, it wasn't hard to figure it out," Jenny replied.

"Let her go, Velima," Cornell said and wondered why she just hadn't changed size and escaped yet. There had to be a reason. "No, you know my terms, give me the heart and she doesn't die, simple right?" Velima asked again. It was clear the voice of reason wasn't going to apply here in the slightest because Jenny's words had no effect at all.

"Okay, fine. I'll get the heart just for you," Cornell finally said. Not willing to risk Jenny's or anyone's life. He'd think of something else later after she was free. "Well, thank you. Everyone said you were kind of immune to this tactic, but this pixie must be special to you. I can't wait to tell all of my friends how to make you do what they want," Velima replied but didn't loosen her grasp on Jenny at all.

Cornell narrowed his eyes at that. He'd kill everyone who targeted her if he had to, but right now he had to do what he said he was going to. A bright red column of fire slammed into Velima's back and knocked her forward. Jenny took the chance and flew straight forward the first chance she got. "I needed to keep her still long enough for that to happen," she said as she landed next to Cornell.

"This was planned?" Cornell asked, surprised that Zozo would help out in any capacity. "No, not planned. I just figured that the good professor here wouldn't let anyone get in his way when he was so close to getting his precious book," Jenny said, her hands lit up with bright golden energy and she fired her own magic into Velima's face, knocking her off her feet.

"Someone, get a stake so we can put an end to this nonsense," Zozo said as he landed, sending more cones of fire down on the vampire's body. Velima was screaming as the red fire ate away at her undead body, but it wasn't screams of pain. It was a word. "Attack," she screamed with a mangled voice.

The darkness around the three of them came to life. Shapes started to emerge, people with glowing red eyes surrounded them pretty quickly. "Vampires," Zozo said and Cornell shook his head, was going to say something but decided to say something else. "Zozo, get us inside the temple, now. I will set up a shield, Hurry," Cornell replied, raised his hands and summoned a red dome of energy around them.

"Fine, I will," Zozo replied, his hands lit up with blue fire and he blasted it at the ground behind the three of them. The flames spread out along invisible lines and formed a square on the ground. Then the square started to rise up out of the dirt at a painstakingly slow pace. The vampires on the outside of the shield began to rip and tear at the energy around it.

"Could you move a little faster, I can only hold back so much here," Cornell said and complained. Each strike against the shield felt like it was against him at the same time.

"It takes as long as it takes, you're a necromancer. Can't you do a little more than, you know, a shield?" Zozo asked. Cornell thought about it, he really hated doing that kind of magic. "I can try to whip up something," Cornell replied, but too late. In his panic he had also left Velima in the shield, and the flames had long since gone out.

She rose from the ashes as she regenerated both her body and clothes at the same time. Cornell didn't have time to think as her pale, clawed hand wrapped around his armored neck. "All of you are going to die now, you're not good enough for immortality. I was going to ask the king to offer it to you, but now, not so much," Velima hissed and picked him up off the ground. Cornell was doing his best to maintain the shield but he was sure that the thing wouldn't last long like this.

Jenny rushed the vampire and grabbed her arms but trying to move them was like trying to move welded steel, no matter how hard she tried, they wouldn't budge. "Little Pixie, you should learn where you came from," Velima said seconds before Jenny blasted her in the face with golden light. It was just enough to make her stumble to the side but not nearly enough.

Zozo thought this was weird. A vampire like this should have been able to kill them all with no trouble, what was all the dramatic showing for. Then something occurred to him. "Red, I don't think we should go in this temple," Zozo said and continued. "You were told this information from a goddess but who's to say any of it was true. We should leave, get out of here. Something isn't right about all of this," he said as the entrance continued to rise.

"We have to trust the Goddess, get inside, now," Cornell said, he couldn't admit now that Zozo might be on to something. They had come too far and through too much to give up now. Besides, the horde of vampires clawing at the shield looked almost feral to him.

"Then we go, now," Zozo said and walked into the entrance, disappearing. Jenny wasted no more time and followed him entrance with blue flames around it. Cornell took off running, the shield fell as he did. The vampires rushed in their direction. Velima didn't know if the entrance would crumble around them or not so she wasted no time and sped into the dark after them, seconds later it closed behind her.

# Chapter Twenty-Two

The entrance to Loa's temple, was not what anyone had expected it to be. It was nothing more than an endless black void. No one could see anyone else and right now there was only silence. All of them were moving by some kind of invisible force.

The situation only lasted just a few seconds. Jenny landed on the warm stone floor and it was as if she had been dropped there. Everything on her insides felt like it had been twisted out of place. Cornell was beside her and it appeared he was feeling the same way. "What in the hell was that?" Jenny managed to ask weakly.

"Loa's entrance to the inner chamber of the temple. It's not for everyone. Get up already you're fine," Zozo replied and she looked at him. He looked just as he always had before. Velima was on her feet as well, but still looked stunned, unaware of where she was. Cornell forced himself to his feet with a groan, everything inside felt off, but that feeling was fading.

He looked around and didn't see any kind of grand cosmic flame. It was just an empty stone, round chamber. "Zozo, where is it?" Cornell asked. Zozo just shrugged. "Last time I was here, there was a massive fire right in the middle of this room. It wasn't like this at all," he replied, just as confused as any of them.

Velima started to laugh at the situation. "All of this work, all of this effort and there isn't a single thing here," she said, still laughing about all of this. Zozo wasn't convinced it was all that different, something had changed but, oh, it occurred to him what changed.

"Loa, I know you can hear me, you sent us here for a reason. We're here, come do your part of the deal," Zozo demanded, but wasn't entirely sure this was the best way to go about it. He supposed confidence was better in the face of cosmic power instead of weakness so he gave it a try.

Jenny wasn't so sure that was a good idea and started backing up towards the wall. Cornell was wondering what Zozo was doing, and he didn't know what was going on either. This all had a planned ending and now, nothing made sense. Maybe the dream was nothing more than just that, a dream. A trick by someone else. Cornell was beginning to feel stupid, and angry and used. Right now, he had half a mind to just hand the heart over just to spite the gods, if they were even real to begin with.

"Okay kids, it's clear the so-called Goddess isn't going to show up. We've played this game long enough. Give me what I want and then we can all leave, come on, what do you say?" Velima asked them again, figuring that now there was no Goddess here. No cosmic fire, nothing but an empty stone chamber forgotten by time built by dead people no one knew anything about.

Cornell sighed. "And when you bring back the King. What then, war starts up, everyone dies or turns into what you are?" he asked, he still didn't like this idea or the vision of the future he had. "Yes, the war never ended. I don't know what happened but that wasn't right. We were going to win, then it all disappeared, we were scattered to the winds," she complained about the past.

"But you're all fine, you have your own Kingdom. You have rights and respect. We accommodate your ways. We have given you so much and some of you still want more?" Jenny asked and was disgusted by the vampire's greed all of the sudden. What made them so special, so deserving of world domination. Nothing, her hands lit up with golden fire as the anger grew.

The four of them stood across from one another, not sure what to do next. Velima prepared for a fight. "Wait," Zozo said suddenly and caught the attention of the others. "Do you see any windows around here, where is the light coming from?" he asked and it was true, the room was sealed, but strangely enough everyone could see everything in the place.

Jenny looked around, but she didn't see anything that looked like a light source either. Everything was the same black stone colored wall. Nothing made sense about this place to her.

"The deal was to bring the heart here to my chamber so it could be destroyed. No one said a vampire was allowed inside," a voice said to them all, it wasn't loud but it did make them jump. "I didn't plan on it, where's the fire so I can do what I came here to do," Cornell replied, but now there was silence.

"Does anyone else feel like we screwed up?" Jenny asked, getting nervous now. "Yeah, I am getting the feeling that Velima over there messed everything up by coming inside this place," Cornell said. Velima took a step back, she sneered but was visibly afraid of what had just happened.

"Silence," the voice said again, angrier this time. Then in the middle of the room a flame erupted, quickly it took form. Loa was standing there before them and the people were too terrified to move. No one has expected any of the Gods to be real but here one was, standing in front of them.

She looked around the four in front of her and crossed her arms. Her thin red dress wrapped around her as if it were made from liquid fire. Loa was taller than everyone here. "The old king can not be brought back. Right now, its too sensitive of a balance. A war would undo everything we have worked to do. It might not have turned out as we planned it but it worked in our favor, give me the heart. I will destroy it now and send you all home," she said and held out her hand.

Cornell was about to do that when a shadow beside him came to life and it was another woman standing beside him, draped in liquid shadow as a dress.

"Or, you could let me have it. I don't fear a war, why should you. The strong need to survive, everything else should be ruled by them," she said and Cornell stepped away in a hurry. "My sister just doesn't appreciate what true power is," she said.

Velima dropped to her knees at once. "Xy, I never thought you were real," she said in a weak, terrified voice. Zozo crossed his arms. "Looks like you have a choice, Red, what are you going to do?" Zozo asked him and Cornell was frustrated.

"Ladies, look. I like the way things are now. We've been without war for a long time and I think I want to keep it that way," he said and Xy turned to look down at him. He could feel her cold gaze through his red armor. "I've always tried to do the right thing and I will continue to do so to protect the world. The old king has to be destroyed," Cornell made his choice and stood by it.

"Well look at that sis, the hero actually does have a spine. He stood up to you despite knowing you could kill him with a touch, impressive," Loa said with a smile. Xy didn't show any emotion at the choice he made. It made Cornell nervous and he was sure that he was going to be turned to dust in about three seconds.

"How about a contest of strength?" Xy asked then and Cornell was relieved that he wasn't going to be dissolved. However, when in the presence of two Goddesses, annoying and whiny was the one thing you really didn't want to be so he was doing his best to keep his cool. He was also thankful for the armor, too.

"What do you have in mind?" Loa asked Xy "Hey, woah you don't want us to fight you, right?" Jenny finally spoke up and the two of them glanced in her direction and Jenny felt her heart sink, realizing that maybe that wasn't such a good idea. "You wouldn't stand a chance against us," Loa replied with a smile.

Her eyes flashed with bright yellow flames as she said that causing Jenny to back off in a hurry.

"I will bring back the King, the best vampire to ever live. The man in red will fight my champion. Then when Jorin wins, the war will resume. Interested, red man?" Xy asked him and Cornell knew next to nothing about the old vampire. "Don't do it, you have no idea the power you will face in combat," Loa said to him.

"Listen to Loa, you can't beat Jorin," Zozo said to him as well. Velima had stood up by now and walked forward. "Fight the king, red man. You can't win and I will prove to you once and for all why this needs to happen," she said but not too forcibly.

"Enough idle chat, what's it going to be?" Loa asked him and crossed her arms. Cornell knew what the right choice was, but either one was going to get him into trouble with the other. Right and wrong no matter made a difference here. The only thing that mattered was being smart, so he made his choice.

"I'll fight your so-called invincible vampire. If he is truly so overpowering as everyone claims, I request another weapon to aid me. I ask for Arket, the Cosmic Flame to help me in the fight," Cornell said, trying to gain favor with Loa and appeasing Xy at the same time, at least he hoped so. The two Goddesses looked at one another and shrugged. "It works for me, you okay with it?" Xy asked.

"Yep, I'm okay with it. However, I'll see if Arket is willing to help. She has a thing about being told what to do and not listening, but I'll ask. Now, if you would go get the heart, we can get this party started," Loa said to him and Cornell still wasn't sure if what he was doing was right. By the looks on everyone's faces he came here with he could tell they thought he was being a massive idiot.

Making up his mind he carved open a hole in the air with his left hand the portal opened. Cornell walked through the portal and they all waited for him to come back.

Zozo walked over to Loa. "Say, you wouldn't happen to have a book around here I could borrow, would you?" he asked, still as confident as ever. She turned and looked at him. "You mean that silly book I wrote ages ago, the one with all the cool secrets of fire in it? The book that has a portal to the elemental plain of fire, that one?" she asked.

"Yeah, that sounds like it," Zozo replied and she shook her head. "No, I'm afraid I've looked into your soul and you've got problems," she said to him and he couldn't help but be disappointed. Jenny breathed a sigh of quiet relief. Then, strangely, he smiled a few seconds later. This didn't make her feel any better.

Xy looked at the vampire, she looked like she about to say something when Cornell stepped back out of the portal and it closed behind him. He had the metal box under his arm. "Give it to me," Xy said and Cornell still couldn't believe what he was doing but it was still the best choice. The last thing he needed was an angry Goddess on his trail for the rest of his life and possibly the rest of eternity.

"Alright, here," he said and handed the metal box to her. Xy took it quickly. "When you all wake up, you'll be ready to face the challenge," Xy said in that same monotone voice. "Wait, what?" Cornell only had time to ask that when all of their vision went black.

# Chapter Twenty-Three

Cornell woke up in his bed. He felt as if he had been sleeping for hours. He knew he had just been on a journey and all of that really happened, but now he was back home. The memory was still fresh, however, even if it was a little bit like a dream. He turned over and Jenny was next to him. He smiled, then hoped Zozo wasn't here in his apartment somewhere too, that would have been weird.

Jenny woke up just seconds after he did. "What is going on?" she asked and he shrugged. "Teleportation, time travel maybe. I don't know for sure," he said and sat up. Thankfully he didn't feel hungover or anything else. Sometimes magic was brutal on the system.

Jenny sat up too. They were both wearing the same clothes they were in the chamber. Jenny reached over for the remote and turned on the television looking for the news. "Holy crap," Jenny said as the screen switched to view of the Western Kingdom's capital city from the air. Sphoric was covered in smoke and rising fire. Jenny turned up the volume.

"All we know is that Unicorns have invaded the city, we don't know how or why but the capital is under siege right now and all we can do is, wait," the camera swung over. "The Unicorn hunters have arrived. Oh, thank Elrox. Commander Mason Rex and his team will surely solve this mess. All we can do now is wait, and watch to see what happens next," the man said and Jenny muted it.

"Mason and the whole team. It really must be a serious situation out there," Cornell said. "You know Rex?" Jenny asked and he shut the television off. "Yeah, we met back some time ago on a case. I thought it was a serial killer, he thought it was a Unicorn. He's a good partner," Cornell said, he knew Rex would be okay.

"Well we need to find a vampire to kill once and for all," Jenny said and Cornell looked at her. "I need to do this, understand?" he said and she drew back a little. "Do you really think I can't help?" she asked and he smiled. "Not that, no. I just don't know if that's part of the rules they set up in the challenge. They might consider it cheating if I had help," he said and she nodded at that. It made sense she supposed.

"Alright then, I'll at least come with you then," Jenny said and Cornell didn't like that idea either but he wasn't stupid enough to argue on this. "You can take care of yourself just fine, and I need the company anyway," he said and smiled.

"I don't know about you but I could use something to eat," Jenny said, realizing the desert meal was hardly enough for anything. "Me too," she replied and knew just the place they could go for what might be their last meal together.

The two of them walked towards the door together. Jenny opened it, almost expecting something else to be there, but there was nothing. She walked out and so did he. Cornell turned around and took one last look at this place. As simple as the place was, it was home. He ran his hand over his pocket to make sure the mirror was still there, it was. He closed the door and locked it.

The two of them walked down the hall. Jenny took him by the hand and their surroundings melted away. Seconds later the outside of Sherrie's Diner came into view. "Teleporting, you know I don't like that," he said and shook off the weird feeling he got when reality melted around him unexpectedly.

"I know but I figure time is running out. The sun is beginning to set and, well, you know how the undead like to work," she said and he rolled his eyes. "Yeah I know, come on let's go in," he replied and the two of them walked inside the place.

"Mr. Nightworth and Ms. Coldwell. Welcome back. It's been a spell since I've seen you two in together, quite the spell," Sherrie said to them a few seconds after they walked in. "Oh, you know. Work is busy and all that," he replied and Sherrie nodded. "Your usual spot in the back is open if you want it," she said and didn't want to take too much of their time. She walked off towards the back.

Jenny and Cornell moved towards their booth in the back and sat down. "Are you sure you didn't make the worst decision on the planet?" Jenny asked him and Cornell shrugged. "If I refused, I would have Xy pissed at me forever or something for breaking her favorite toy. I figured it was the best thing I could do at the time," he replied, but looked sad about it.

"I guess you're right. That doesn't mean I have to like it," she said and was frustrated. He was going to say something else when someone else came to their table. A woman dressed in typical desert tourist wear with dark brown eyes and red hair, wearing a red t-shirt and blue shorts, neither items of clothes fit right, they were too tight. "Cornell Nightworth?" she asked and he shook his head.

"Uh, yeah," he said, it was clear Cornell didn't know her at all. "May I join you two people for a quick second?" she asked and he just looked at Jenny for help here. She didn't know what to do either, it was a very strange situation. "Sure," he said and slid over.

The stranger sat down next to him. "Hi, nice to meet you. I'm Arket. Loa asked me really nice to come talk to you, so I did. I have to say I like this place a lot better than up north," she said and Cornell was stunned. He was expecting Arket to be an actual sword, not a person.

Jenny tilted her head. "How?" she was going to ask more but Arket cut her off in a hurry. "Nothing you need to worry about, it's a long story and not important. I'm just here to see if you're worth my time or not," she replied and Cornell realized that Sherrie hadn't come back yet. Actually, now that he looked around, he realized that all of time had stopped around them. Everyone was frozen in place.

"I am sure you know all the details," Cornell replied and Arket nodded. "It seems you have a vampire problem and you think you need my help to take him out," she said. "Yeah, I could do it on my own I think, but I figured since Loa was involved. She'd feel bad If I didn't, you know, ask for her help," Cornell replied.

"Yeah, they can get kind of touchy about things like that. But you said you can fight the thing on your own, that's the kind of confidence I like in a guy. I'll help you out," she said to him with a smile. There was something about this smile that gave both of them the chills. Cornell's world had exploded in the past few days. Things he always thought were mere myths were true. This made him think that the situation of the Northern Kingdom was much more serious than he first thought.

"Thank you," Cornell said and Arket drew back to lean against the booth. "Thank me after we win," she replied to him and Cornell nodded.

"I have questions," Jenny said then breaking up the conversation. Arket looked at her and the smile disappeared. "You might have questions, but really I don't have any answers. My whole world was turned upside down. I have literally nothing to do. I used to possess the body of a Princess, now I am just a wanderer like the rest of my family. I have no answers for you," she said with a hint of depression.

Jenny shook her head. "I was just going to ask if you wanted something to eat. Not for your whole life story," she replied and Arket got a blank look on her face. "Oh, I see, generally I don't eat anything. I'm just a sword and all," she replied.

"Best looking sword I've ever seen," Cornell said without thinking, then Jenny punched Cornell in the arm. "Watch it," she said. "Ouch," he said and rubbed his arm. Arket couldn't help but laugh at the two of them.

"Well, I can only keep time stopped for so long, the sun is going down and by now Xy's boy toy should be back in one piece, we should get going," she said to them. "If you want to stay safe you should leave the city or find somewhere safe," Arket said to her. "Leave the city, really?" she asked, sarcastically.

"It could get pretty ugly, its up to you," Arket replied. Jenny and Cornell looked at one another. "No, you need to get to headquarters and warn everyone that there is bad stuff coming, no, scratch that. Go to the castle and warn them," Cornell said to Jenny.

Jenny nodded. "Yeah, that feels like a good plan. I just hope they believe me," she said and he shook his head. "Of course, they'll believe you, and if they don't just wait until the explosions start. That should change their mind," Cornell said and tried to smile.

"Alright, we need to go now, come with me," Arket said and stood up. Cornell kissed Jenny, then slid out of the booth. "See you soon," he said. "You know I will, be safe and win," Jenny replied. "With a cosmic sword on my side I can't lose," Cornell replied, then with one last look the two of them walked out of the diner. Jenny teleported away seconds later.

Sherrie came to the booth and was completely confused as to why they were both suddenly missing when they were only there a minute ago.

# Chapter Twenty-Four

Cornell and Arket walked down a sidewalk. There were other people out and about but no one paid any attention to them. "So, where are we going?" Cornell asked. "It's not far now, come on," she replied and he didn't like all the secrecy all of the sudden. All of this was beginning to feel like some kind of an elaborate trap.

The two of them turned a corner into an alley. At the end a tall figure was standing there, he was looking at his hands as if he hadn't seen them in a long time. Then he noticed them and started walking in their direction. The first thing Cornell noticed about the guy was his glowing white eyes. He wasn't sure if he should attack or what. Besides the strange eyes, nothing seemed aggressive about him.

"Stay back for a minute, Arket. If anything, bad or terrible happens come help, otherwise maybe this won't be so bad," he said and she crossed her arms. "It's your funeral, but sure. I'll hang back for a bit. I should warn you, I can see the dark energies rolling off this guy. He's leagues beyond any vampire I've ever seen in my travels," she said and Cornell steeled his nerves with this information. "At the first sign of trouble, you know what to do," Cornell said and started walking in his direction to meet him.

"Hello. You must be Cornell Nightworth," he said and held out his hand to shake it. Cornell didn't know what to do and he wished that not everyone knew his name before he told them what it was. He imagined the minute he took his hand, his arm being ripped off in a second, it was possible. Cornell took the chance and grabbed his hand. "Yep, that's me," he replied with the firmest hand shake he could possibly give, he doubted Jorin even felt it. The hand shake only lasted a few seconds.

"Jorin Idris, Nice to meet you," he said and this was nothing what Cornell expected at all. "So, I actually never expected to see anything ever again," he said and Cornell just shrugged a little. "Apparently a few people think you're going to make everything right again," Cornell said and Jorin shook his head and stepped into the rays of the dying sun still filtering through in the alley way.

"Everything is right. This is exactly what I wanted. Vampires have a home, they aren't being hunted by the rest of the world anymore. They are respected as citizens of the world by most people," Jorin said and smiled. The sunlight didn't burn his skin in the slightest as he stood in it.

"Well, alright then. What are we going do now? I mean if I can avoid a fight with the most powerful vampire the world has ever known in recent memory, I'd be good with that," Cornell said and Jorin looked at him. "Not even a friendly spar. I hear you have the Mirror of Osan, I'd like to test that power out against my own. I knew Osan back when we went to school, I always wondered what happened to him. I suppose he died after I got bit at some point," Jorin said with a hint of sadness in his voice.

Cornell took his mirror out of his pocket. "This thing is supposed to be four hundred years old, maybe more. And you knew the guy who made this when he was a kid?" Cornell asked and Jorin smiled. "I wasn't always the king, you know," he said as he looked at the thing.

"Fine, I guess we can put on a good show for them. They are expecting a fight. But if you win Xy will think you will restart the war," Cornell said and Jorin smiled. "Two things. First, no one tells me what to do, second, the war is over. I found a way for everyone to win and I think I need to keep it that way," he replied and Cornell shrugged, he figured this might all turn out better than he thought.

"Shall we engage in combat then?" Jorin asked and Cornell opened his mirror, red electric sparks wrapped around him and he returned to his armored form. "What, no cape, Osan loved capes," Jorin said and Cornell sighed. "There is one but, I don't know. I never liked it," he replied and released it. The cape exploded. It wasn't cloth, instead it was pure red energy that held its form. "Osan also liked the color red, maybe a bit too much," Jorin admitted.

"Yeah, I think so too," Cornell said just as the sun disappeared from the alleyway. Cornell shot into the sky, with the electric cape he looked more like a bolt of energy as he did. Jorin flew up into the sky to meet him.

Jorin looked over the whole city and seemed impressed at what he saw. "I know you want to check the place out but let's get this over with," Cornell said and Jorin nodded. "You go first," he replied and Cornell hadn't ever been in a fight quite like this before. Usually it was always a surprise attack and it was over pretty quick.

Cornell made a fist with his left hand and decided to go for it. He swung at the vampire's head. Jorin caught his fist as if it were little more than falling paper, spun around and tossed him through the sky with ease. "You get a free shot and you lead with that, I have to say I am a little disappointed," Jorin said and almost laughed about it.

Cornell stopped himself and wondered what he should do next. Of course, sparing with on of the the most powerful vampire kings, maybe he could stand to let loose a little bit. His hands lit up with red energy. Jorin was far away one minute, then mere feet in front of him in a flash. "Now, buddy. I know that armor has more magic in that thing, right?" he asked and

Cornell honestly didn't know. He used the armor more like a gun than anything else.

"I suppose it does. Most of the people I go against are idiots. There is no reason to go all out on someone who can barely figure out how to work a basic cell phone and spends most of their time high on Ice brain," he replied, still trying to make a plan here.

Jorin didn't know what a cell phone was but that was okay, he didn't care. In his moment of distraction Cornell blasted Jorin in the face with the red energy at point blank range. Jorin turned his head as his skin sizzled, but that was all he did in response.

When the light faded, Jorin turned to look at him and smiled. This time his smile was not friendly. "That was just enough to get the fire started," Jorin said, grabbed Cornell's wrists. On physical contact, the armor let loose a great amount of electrical energy reacting with the King's own natural power. Jorin didn't pay attention to it and with his free hand he punched Cornell in the stomach so hard that the impact sounded like thunder.

"Are you still alive inside there or did I break your everything?" Jorin asked. Cornell had never been hit that hard before. He was thankful the armor protected him from that attack but now wasn't the time to dwell on it. He pulled away from the vampire and punched him in the stomach to return the favor, this time the attack landed and Jorin doubled over. The second he did, he put his right hand into the back of Jorin's neck sending him flying towards the ground.

Cornell grunted, he knew this magic was stronger than it looked and now it looked like he would have to find out just how far he could go with it. He raced down out of the sky to go and find Jorin, but when he got there, there was no sign of him anywhere.

"Did I hit you too hard and you just fell apart when you hit the ground or what?" Cornell asked, almost disappointed. There was no answer, once again the longer he stood here in this alleyway, the more and more he felt like this was all a big trap. "I know all magic reflects from the armor. Osan was obsessed with defensive magic, that was his biggest dream he ever had, so my magic skills won't be much use directly against you," Jorin said and continued. "However, I thought of a nifty work around," he said from nowhere.

Cornell spun around expecting something to be there but it was just a wall. This friendly sparring session felt less friendly by the second. Then a section wall behind him tore off and slammed him into the other side of the alley. His armor saved him from being smashed but still, he was pinned in place now. His hands exploded with red energy and the wall was shredded with power, turning to dust around him.

Jorin was standing there and grabbed by the neck as soon as he turned around. "You know. I do have to admit I am kind of disappointed," he said and lifted Cornell off his feet. "I really expected more out of you. I could tear you to pieces at any time I wanted, I think," he said to him. "You could try," Cornell replied and knew that the only way to actually stand a chance he had to fight more like a mage and less like a detective.

Cornell summoned his necromantic energies inside of him and channeled it through the armor as the vampire held him in the air pale green and blue streaks of energy erupted through the red armor plating. The flash of light caused Jorin to drop him and shield his eyes for a second. He took that time to kick the vampire into the hole he made. "Alright, now we can get down to business," he said to himself. Of course, he had no idea just hat he was really getting into here, he had a feeling that this was nothing more than child's play to Jorin after all and there was no possible way that he could win here, not like this anyway.

# Chapter Twenty-Five

Jenny was approaching the front gate to the castle. She was sill trying to figure out just what to say, she'd never talked to anyone like this before, there was never any need to and she was pretty nervous about it. She took a deep breath, finalizing on what to say. "Hey, come here," a voice said to her from the side and she stopped, turned and looked. It was Zozo, but he was in street clothes. Without his green cloak he was almost unrecognizable.

Jenny still wasn't sure about trusting him but she turned and walked towards him anyway. "What happened to you?" she asked him in a hurry. "I don't know. I woke up back where I started and figured at least one of you would come here to warn the royals," he replied and continued. "Are you sure you want to do that?" he asked her.

Jenny thought about it and didn't see what the big problem was by doing it. "Why not?" he asked and Zozo almost laughed. "How do people in power react when a potential threat to their own power shows up?" he asked and Jenny realized exactly what happens, and imagined a whole lot worse.

"Okay, I get you," she replied and looked at the castle. "So, let Cornell handle it, give him a chance to do it and maybe, just maybe we'll be okay," Zozo replied. Jenny became suspicious. "I don't know you all that well, but why are you being so, helpful?" she asked him. "Why did you save me in Larenville from the creeps, you didn't need to kill them," she added. Zozo just smirked at that, ignored it and proceeded to answer her first question.

"Well, I want to be the one to kill Cornell. He has it coming. Secondly, I think that maybe nothing is what it seems around here. I think that the revival of the old King is someone else's plan. Think about it. How much do we actually know besides the obvious reasons?" Zozo asked her. Jenny thought about it. It was true, the only reason for reviving Jorin was weak at best. To revive the war no one seemed to actually want on either side.

"Jenny, come on you need to see that something doesn't make sense, everything's been entirely too easy up until this point," Zozo said and she had to agree with that. A vampire like Velima should have been able to rip them all to pieces or at least be a bigger threat than she was. Instead it felt like nothing more than a push in the right direction this whole time.

Footsteps coming from behind them attracted their attention. The both of them turned around and saw Velima walking in their direction. "You two are really stupid for standing out here in the open like this. Any vampire can track you down with ease," she said to them as she got closer. Jenny and Zozo prepared for a fight.

"Calm down, I'm not here to kill you. If I was you'd be dead already," Velima replied to them. Jenny supposed that was true. "What do you want. You're the reason for all of this. Who are you?" Jenny asked her. "Oh look. Now the detective is asking all the big questions. I'm not sure if I should be disappointed or depressed it took you this long," Velima replied.

Jenny was sure she asked before, but so much had happened that it was hard to remember all the details. "It's been foretold that the time was right for Old Stone tooth to give the blessing of Xy. Someone there is going to receive the blessing of Xy when it's all said and done the vampire kingdom is going to have a new leader," Velima said and continued. "Tradition says that only one Xy blessed vampire can exist on the planet at one time. I was trying to make sure that it was Jorin and not some soft rookie who will lead the Morglands into ruin. We can't afford that," she replied.

"Wait, all of this is done because of some Prophecy?" Zozo asked and Velima shrugged. "It's better to be safe than sorry, don't you think?" she asked and Zozo cringed at that statement. "No, you idiot. Sometimes it's better to just leave well enough alone. I'm pretty sure being a heart in a box somewhere hardly counts as existing. Now Jorin is, well, alive I guess. If your prophecy comes true then you just screwed everything up," Zozo replied to her. Jenny laughed.

"You did all of this because you didn't trust that someone new might, or might not be better than the one you knew in the past. How human of you," she said. The situation wasn't funny in the least but right now, once it was all brought to light. Jenny found it kind of pathetic. "I figure if Jorin was walking around, the blessing of Xy wouldn't be given to anyone else. Also, since the blade incident in the north, the Gods have returned, you saw them. I can't risk some loser being chosen as the new ruler of the Kingdom," she said.

"You're an idiot," Zozo replied and turned to face the city. "Now we have the strongest one of you facing down someone who has no idea what the true limits of his power is somewhere in the city. Do you know how many people you might have killed," Zozo asked, Jenny was surprised he cared, but before she asked she figured it was because this was just less people he would get to kill in the future or something like that.

"Well, we should try and stop them before they wreck the whole city tonight," Jenny suggested and Velima nodded. "Yeah, that feels like the right thing to do. There aren't many vampires in Echemos but once they sense the energy of the old King there is no telling how they might react," Velima replied and that worried the others. The three of them decided to go search for the two fighters and see if they could stop the battle.

They took off into the night air and quickly soared over the city, looking for signs of a fight, but right now, from up here there was nothing they could see that was obvious. "Come on, this way," Velima said and flew to the east. The other two didn't bother questioning her right now because they knew she could feel Jorin's energy from almost anywhere.

# Chapter Twenty-Six

Cornell's new strategy of focusing his own energy through the armor was working. He punched Jorin in the face while his fist crackled with deep red energy and knocked him to the ground. "You're not so tough, I bet all the kids picked on you in school, too," Cornell said to him but then wondered If that was a mistake. Maybe that was the berserk button and would set him off from just playing around to dismembering people without a second thought.

Jorin laughed as he hit the ground "They did," he replied to him. "Oh, how they did, but that doesn't matter now," Jorin replied and smiled. Finally, his enemy was putting up a little bit of a fight and using his head, too. "This is fun and all but I think we need to turn it up a notch, don't you think?" Jorin asked with a smile.

"What now?" Cornell replied and just as he said that, Jorin was behind him and punched Cornell in the back of the neck but before he could fall the vampire caught his left arm and slammed him into the brick building face first. Cornell smashed through it and screaming immediately commenced from the people on the other side. "Oh, my bad," Jorin said as the family scrambled to get out of the way.

A section of wall was pinning and older Elf to the floor. Jorin hovered over the man. He looked down at the terrified one and smiled. The white eyed King reached down and pulled the wall up. "Leave," he said as he held the wall up. The man scrambled away in a hurry. The wall fell to the ground after he was clear of it.

"All of you, leave," Jorin commanded in a much deeper, powerful voice than he had been using up until now. The elves scrambled out of their ruined apartment as fast as they could. "I'm surprised you didn't just eat them," Cornell said as he managed to stand up.

"Elves taste terrible. Its something about all the magic in their blood stream," Jorin said and shrugged. "I guess if I get hungry enough next time they won't be so lucky," Jorin added and Cornell charged him, knocking him back outside into the alleyway. He didn't want to destroy anything if he could help it but this felt like it was becoming impossible. Jorin didn't care in the slightest about keeping things intact and stopped himself and Cornell, sliding his feet against the cement floor.

"You seem to be getting stronger as you fight. Good," Jorin said and took off into the air, holding Cornell. "We need to fight where we can be seen. Let the world know we exist," Jorin said and Cornell didn't like the sound of that but now he didn't have much of a choice in the matter. The two of them flew apartment's side and right over the top in three seconds.

Then Jorin threw him straight back down into the street below, the pavement broke to pieces when he landed on it. There were elves on the sidewalk who had been attracted by the sudden noise behind the building. Now they were witness to something not too many people believe existed. Jorin landed on the street and a few feet away from him and the eyes of the crowd turned on him.

Jorin didn't bother to take notice of them but he did see a large car sitting on the side of the road. The vampire walked and stood beside it. He put his left hand on the front of it, crunched the metal in his hand to get a good grip on it. He picked the thing up and threw it at Cornell as if it were weightless. Cornell reacted immediately reacted the only way he could.

Cornell steeled himself and caught it. It was heavy, but not as much as he was expecting it to be but he didn't plan on holding it very long. He twisted the thing and sat it down on its tires. Without missing a beat, he flew over the car and attacked the vampire yet again, but he was still moving at his normal speed. Jorin just stepped back with ease and put his knee into Cornell's chest knocking him straight back and into the air.

"You still fight like an elf, but you should fight like someone who has actual power, you keep holding yourself back, why?" Jorin asked him and was getting frustrated. Cornell never had many good reasons to push himself. As he thought about an answer Jorin grabbed him by the left wrist and threw him back down into the pavement, breaking it even further. Cornell thought he could feel his inside being turned into mush right about now.

If there was any good time to push his limits, he supposed now was a good time. He pushed the thoughts of innocent people getting in the way out of his mind and charged in his direction. Up until now the vampire had just been playing with him, that ended now if he could help it. He was going to give it is all and dig deeper than ever before.

Cornell pushed himself up off the ground and closed the distance in a second, grabbed Jorin by the throat. The iron flesh of the vampire turned soft in his grip for the first time. With his right hand he punched the vampire in the chest and the two of them flew into the night sky. "Fine, I'll tear you apart," Cornell said in his altered voice and fully intended on doing just that.

He had to win to save the world from a war it couldn't win. Jorin grabbed Cornell's wrist, pulled it away from his neck. This time it took a considerable amount of effort. "Now it's a fight, I hope," he said, still sounding unimpressed with the whole event.

Instead of falling back to the ground, Jorin took control of the flight and shot straight up at blinding speeds.

Cornell had never been this high before. The sprawling metropolis of Echemos now just looked like the black sands of the desert they had seen before from up here. "Take one last look at your precious city. I wanted you to see it one last time, in its entire form. No matter who wins here between us, it's going to be destroyed," Jorin said and Cornell had no idea what that meant, nor did he care.

The red armor exploded with energy and he pulled away from the monster. He wondered if he could ever hurt this thing like this, really hurt it. Jorin smiled at him. "Would you like a taste of the power you're up against?" he asked and Cornell felt a little fear for the first time. He was thankful that his armor hid the expression that must have been on his face right now.

"I'll take your silence as a yes, please. So, watch me work," Jorin said with a smile, still never revealing his fangs, however. Cornell felt a chilling wind blow right through his armor as Jorin's eyes burned bright white. The moon and the stars above them began to be blocked out by a sickly green cloud that began to form above him. "What?" Cornell asked himself, barely realizing it he did as he stood in awe of the thing.

"This hasn't been seen in a century, this is the King's shroud. It signals the beginning of undead Dominance in the world. Any vampire who sees this and is loyal will know the war has returned and everyone with a pulse is fair game," Jorin said and as he did a thick, bright blue bolt of lightning struck Cornell and in an instant, he hit the roof of a skyscraper. Cracking the roof of the thing on impact he felt like his body had been fried. Whatever power this was, it wasn't magic, his armor took the full blast and he couldn't move.

Cornell could only stare up into the sky as the green mist continued to spread in all directions. He was sure that he was beaten, there was no way he could do it alone. "Okay. I tried and

I know I'm outmatched. If I'm not, I don't have time to find the inner power I need to fight. Arket, I think I could use your help now," he said, trying to catch his breath.

"I was wondering when you were going to ask. I was going to help right away but I figured you'd want to do your elf pride, man thing and go it alone at first. I know how you mortals work," Arket replied to him as she walked across the roof. "Yeah, you know I had to at least try it," he replied, but still felt like he was made of stone right now.

She rolled her red eyes and transformed into her weapon form with a red blaze. Arket floated into Cornell's hand and he grasped the hilt. Her cosmic fire flowed through his armor and into him. He sat straight up. "Wow," he said looking at the burning blade in his hand. "You do know I could take you over anytime I wanted, right?" Arket asked him and that made him have a reality check. "Yeah. I know, thanks for not doing that, but how are you not being reflected right now?" he asked and held the blade out in front of him. "I asked not to be and the mirror agreed," she said and all the sudden Cornell felt a little creeped out.

"I'm not much of a sword guy. I like guns if anything," he said and was entranced by Arket's multi colored flame. "Well, deal with it and I'll try not to be too offended," she replied to him and Cornell cringed a little and made a mental note to watch what he said a little closer from now on. With that the two of them took off into the swirling green sky.

# Chapter Twenty-Seven

Arket and Cornell flew up to the tiny speck of black in the sky. Jorin was still there, and neither of them knew what he was doing, nor did they care. The second the two of them got level with him. Jorin backed off in a hurry. "Arket, how did you get that blade?" he asked and for the first time sounded worried.

"Shut up and fight us," Cornell said, but Arket's voice said as they blended together. Jorin didn't know how he was going to fight a literal weapon of the Gods and all of the sudden this was really unfair to him and he knew it.

"You know, back in the day I held Ventrix. I never used the weapon because as much as I wanted to win, I never wanted to doom the world in the process," Jorin said as he stared at the burning blade. "Looks like I was a fool back then. Someone unleashed the blades and everyone is still here," he said sadly, thinking about what could have been. Then he shook his head and focused on right now.

"Fine," Jorin replied and the green mist swirled around Jorin's body then. Cornell didn't care what was going on. Arket pointed herself to the sky and blasted her fire into the sky. The thousand colored flame dispersed the mist on contact and burned it out of the sky. Cornell took off and time froze. Jorin was still moving but so slowly that it was surprising. "This really is unfair," Cornell said. "No fight is fair, if you think this is fast you should see my sister go. Lumic makes me look like I'm standing still," Arket replied to him just as fast.

Cornell decided that maybe Jorin was worthy to redeem after all. He hadn't hurt anyone and even went out of his way to save people. He kicked the vampire in the back and in a flash, he was gone leaving a trail of dark green smoke leading back towards the city. "Just kill him and call it a day," Arket said to him inside his head. "I don't think he's that bad of a guy anymore, I need to discover the truth for myself," Cornell replied and followed the green trail all the way down from high above to the street in just a few seconds.

Jorin was pulling himself out of the crater he made in the street. The surrounding buildings all had their windows broken out and small fires had started, too. Jorin walked out of the crater and brushed off the dust he had on him. If he was hurt, there was no indication. "I need to know what you plan to do if I let you live?" Cornell asked him.

All he had to do was win the fight, he didn't remember anyone saying anything about killing him. Just winning, he could do that. "Do, I want to do what anyone does, disappear. If Arket is free the other blades are free as well. This can only mean the world is coming to an end maybe not now but things will change. I want no part of it," he said and Cornell believed him, well, most of it.

"On the other hand, I have to admit things do seem weird lately, but we need to come up with a plan now because there are goddesses out there who are waiting for an outcome, and I doubt they are going to wait long so we need to come up with an arrangement and fast," Cornell said and Jorin looked away from Cornell.

"Kill me then, and end it, I never wanted to be here in the first place. This world has no room for someone like me in it anymore," Jorin said and Cornell shook his head. "I've got a better idea," he said. But before he could finish, footsteps approached them.

They turned to look and it was Zozo and Jenny and Velima approaching them. "Great, what are they doing here?" Cornell asked no one "Jorin, I'm sorry for causing so much trouble," Velima said, it sounded more like a plea for mercy. Cornell was confused. What happened since they were fighting?

"I suppose you know of the prophecy too and panicked, right?" Jorin said and Velima's blue eyes went wide and she looked down. "Yes," she replied. All of this was new to Cornell, but right now he had a pressing problem.

"Great, but what are we going to do now, about the Goddesses?" Cornell said and Zozo nodded. "I have come up with a plan for that, but you're going to have to trust me," he said and smiled. Cornell didn't trust this guy, but up until now he hadn't stabbed him in the back.

"We just cover it up, if our blade friend here is willing to help," he said and glanced towards Arket. "Someone please do something, or I'll kill you all right here," she replied and Zozo took that as a yes.

"Cover it up how?" Jorin asked. "It's easy, I'll make you into a 'mere mortal' it's basically an illusion spell but all we need to do is cast it the moment you die, well, 'die' is a bit extreme but you need to look like you're dead to fool you know who, so interested?" Zozo asked and Jorin shrugged. "Either you fake kill me and I go away or you mess up and I really die, either way works for me," he replied and Zozo smiled.

"Let us prepare and you two make it look good, five minutes from now bring the fight back here and stab Jorin here in the chest, close to the heart, all the way through. We'll do the rest, go," Zozo said to them. With no warning at all Jorin stepped around Arket and the two of them disappeared into the sky.

"Alright ladies, let's get to work," Zozo said and hoped they could get everything they needed done in five minutes. He was worried that that might not be enough time after all.

"Do you trust him?" Jorin asked as they flew through the night. "Not a chance, but he's a lot like you are now. Just wants to be left alone I think these days. So, I guess this time we can," Cornell said and as he did Jorin threw him onto the roof of another building. Cornell landed on his feet, annoyed, then came up with an idea. "Wait. If we're going to fight and blow stuff up, can we make it useful?" Cornell asked and Jorin crossed his arms. "What did you have in mind?" he asked.

"The Moreno family, the mob. Criminal scum has warehouses and secret places all over the city. We can't get them all but do you think we could clean some house?" Cornell asked and Jorin knew he was smiling. "There is no greater threat to any kingdom than the criminal element that would eat it from the inside out, lead the way, Mr. Nightworth," Jorin replied with a smile.

"I'm finally going to get to do something fun, I can't wait," Arket said and it sounded like she was smiling at least. "Follow me," Cornell said and took off into the air to the west. It didn't take them very long but they were over the warehouse district of the city. Cornell pointed at the one in the back, towards the edge of the lot. "Throw me into that one," he said.

Jorin grabbed him by the back of the neck, spun him around and tossed him straight towards it. Cornell tore through the metal roof and hit the cement. "Maybe not get thrown so hard next time," he said as he stood up slowly. Sure enough the place was filled with boxes of all shapes and sizes, stacked high above his head. He punched a hole through the box he was closest to and pulled out a bag full of purple powder. He tossed it to the ground. "Chill weed," he said to himself.

Seconds later Jorin flew through the roof and saw the bag. "Night's Breath?" he asked and Cornell hadn't heard that term for it used for it. "This place is filled with it, that and who knows what else. Let's burn the whole place to the ground," Cornell said and Arket exploded with fire. She was a little too eager for destruction. The blast wave spread out so far, and was so powerful that both Cornell and Jorin were knocked to the ground.

Cornell sat up and the only thing around him he could see was fire. "Holy," Cornell said as he saw his surroundings. The sky was deep red and the flames rose high. "What did you do?" Jorin asked as he walked out of a fire, his hair was singed but otherwise he was doing alright. "I destroyed it," she said, the two of them stood in a crater and half the warehouses were vaporized.

"Damn, woman a little warning next time," Cornell said, mostly to himself. "You wanted to clean house, consider the house cleaned," Arket replied and Jorin shook the ash from his clothes. "Has it been five minutes yet?" he asked, looking at the devastation around them.

"No, anyone else you need to visit," Jorin asked and Cornell wished he knew where the head of the Moreno family was so he could cut it off, but he didn't and that was just too bad. "No, but we need to get out of here before we attract the wrong kinds of attention," Cornell said and took to the air. Just a few feet into the air and he was concealed by all the smoke. Jorin followed him. They looked down at what Arket had done and there was nothing left but a large crater in the ground where the warehouses used to be.

"Come on, we've done enough. Let's go back to Zozo and see what he has planned," Cornell said, he had no idea if it was five minutes or not but it felt long enough to him. "If you say so, I just hope what ever he has planned works," Arket replied. The three of them shot away from the scene, leaving the mass destruction behind.

# Chapter Twenty-Eight

Jorin and Cornell made their way back to where they started, but no one was here waiting for them. "What the hell?" Cornell asked as they landed. "Don't you mean where?" Jorin asked right away and Cornell didn't bother replying to that. He looked around but still, he didn't see anything that might have let them know where they might have gone.

Jorin came walking up behind them. "I found this," he said and handed it to Cornell. It was a note. Cornell took one look at it, all it said on it was 'Trust me, sword in the chest, make it look real. We'll do the rest,' he read and the paper turned to ash just after he read it.

"I trust you, do you trust me?" Arket said and Jorin shrugged. "Either way I win, let's do this," he replied. Cornell didn't know just how much the gods knew and didn't know. He figured they were watching this whole time, anyway.

"Alright, vampire edge lord, prepare to die," Cornell said, not really knowing what else to say. "Edge lord, really?" Jorin replied and took a step back as he turned around. Cornell shrugged a little and swung Arket in his direction, it was a sloppy swing that Jorin barely had to move to avoid. "Oh yeah, you paladin wannabe, I shall smite you with the full power of the undead hordes," Jorin replied and if they were acting over the top, he decided to play along for now and thrust himself forward. Jorin's fist slammed into the left side of Cornell's head and knocked him off his feet and into the wall.

"Wow," Cornell said to himself, even with his armor on that attack hurt. "Get up," Arket said to him, tired of laying against the wall. Cornell listened to her and stood back up. "Die, fiend," he yelled and ran in his direction, intending to strike the last blow now. Jorin didn't catch the intention and dodged to the left. As Cornell passed by he caught him by the back of the neck, picked him up only to slam him face first into the cement, shattering pieces of it in the process.

Cornell grunted in pain and frustration. "Damn it, you undead worm, you were supposed to die, I'll get you next time," he said and Jorin picked him right back up and held Cornell off the ground at face level. "You can't hurt me, not even with that magic toothpick you call a sword," Jorin said and immediately regretted it. He had no idea if cosmic powered, sentient weapons could understand sarcasm that well.

"You called me a toothpick?" Arket said and exploded with golden fire. Cornell lost control of his arm. Arket rose up and covered Cornell with deep red and black fire. "Toothpick," she said in a deeper, angrier voice. Before either of them could react Arket plunged herself deep into Jorin's chest at lightning speed.

Jorin looked down at the burning blade. "Thanks," he said with a smile and white light exploded from his body in all directions. Cornell shielded his eyes for a second. When he could see again, Jorin was gone. There weren't even any ashes to be seen. He could feel Arket's anger and control fading away. "Not a word," Cornell said, he didn't know if that was the plan or that was how vampire King's died.

"I'm out of here before any other cosmic beings show up. It was nice working with you," Arket said and Cornell let her go, she shot up into the night sky and disappeared. The fire around his body went out and Arket's power left him. The effect of the loss was felt immediately and he fell to his knees.

A column of fire descended beside him. "You won, I knew you had it in you, champ," Loa said and Cornell still didn't have enough energy to stand up straight yet. "The vampire, you know, he wasn't all that bad," Cornell said between breaths.

"No one is all bad. You, doing what you do should know that by now. But the vampire had too much power to be allowed to run free. Eventually the urge to go back to the war days would be listened to. All the undead of such power tend to seek dominance without something to temper their fierce nature. You save the world today, at least. In a sense," Loa said to him, put her hand on his shoulder.

Cornell felt his strength return, but when he looked around the Goddess was gone. "Thank you," he said to no one, but was sure she was still listening somewhere. Now he expected Xy to show up and obliterate him in an instant. He was worried, but the darkness around him didn't come to life and strangle him. Everything was, with any luck, back to normal.

"I'm going home," he said to himself and took off into the sky and faded into the shadow realm. From here he could see the massive destruction from here, smoke still rose high into the night sky. He couldn't help but smile and wished he could see Moreno's face right now when he learned that countless tons of his supply went up in smoke. Then he supposed that this would just be seen as a minor setback to scum like that.

Ignoring it, he flew to his apartment building and phased through the wall. Once he got there he rematerialized back into the physical world and transformed back to his normal form. Then he noticed his lights were on and the shower was running. He supposed it was Jenny but it could have been anyone for all he knew, it was always a bad idea to assume anything.

He slowly opened the door and peeked inside. There was a female form behind the curtain barely visible. He knew that form anywhere and carefully stepped back outside and sat on the bed. He had quite eventful couple of days. In an effort not to think about it, he turned on the television, it was the news. He had expected to see live coverage of the fires. Instead, he saw something else.

"It is a warzone here in Sphoric, the unicorn invasion is being brought under control. Reports are coming in that Commander Rex of the Elite Unicorn Hunter team is missing in action. Nothing is confirmed at this time. We can only hope for the best possible outcome here, more details to follow," the man said as the screen only showed the city below, the place looked like an actual war had broken out.

Cornell was worried about that but as soon as he heard the bathroom door opened, he shut the television off. This was the last thing Jenny needed to see or worry about right now. "Hey," she said and smiled, wrapped in a white towel.

He looked at her and smiled. "We're alone now, so, did it work?" Cornell asked and Jenny walked and sat beside him. "I don't know. Zozo said that only he would know and he could shield his thoughts from the Gods. Don't ask how because I don't know," she said and continued. "Said it was safer if we didn't know for sure," she said and he smiled. "And the vampire?" he asked her.

"She flew off just after the spell worked, I hope we don't need to worry about her anymore, we'll let someone else chase her down for what she did to the outpost," she said and he sighed "I guess we can give her a couple days head start," he said and pulled her back on the bed and they both lay there. They were both too tired to worry about it now.

Jenny smiled for a second, snapped her fingers and the lights turned off enveloping the room in darkness. Tomorrow's problems could wait until then. For now, all was well.

Dear reader,

We hope you enjoyed reading *Red Mirror*. Please take a moment to leave a review, even if it's a short one. Your opinion is important to us.

Discover more books by Jesse Wilson at
https://www.nextchapter.pub/authors/jesse-wilson

Want to know when one of our books is free or discounted? Join the newsletter at http://eepurl.com/bqqB3H

Best regards,

Jesse Wilson and the Next Chapter Team

You could also like:

Cradle of the Gods by Thomas Quinn Miller

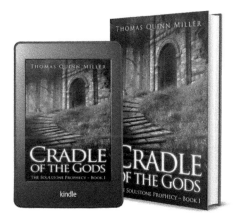

To read the first chapter for free, please head to:
https://www.nextchapter.pub/books/cradle-of-the-gods-epic-
fantasy-adventure

Lightning Source UK Ltd.
Milton Keynes UK
UKHW022009061120
372956UK00003B/320